THE DEVIL BEATS HIS WIFE

To order additional copies, please contact us.
BookSurge, LLC
www.booksurge.com
1-866-308-6235
orders@booksurge.com

HORACE MUNGIN

THE DEVIL BEATS HIS WIFE

AND OTHER STORIES FROM THE LOWCOUNTRY

2004

THE DEVIL BEATS HIS WIFE

CONTENTS

ACKNOWLEDGEMENTS

Special thanks to: Barbara Lewis, Geraldine Mungin and Alicia White.

AUTHOR'S NOTE

Once, while I was laid up sick in bed, my sister Barbara brought me a collection of short stories – I think the title was "Studies in the Short Story." It was a book she had to read for her high school English class. The anthology contained stories by the great fiction writers from around the world, from nineteenth century Fedor Dostroevshi to twentieth century James Baldwin. Oh, what a marvelous book. I first read it merely to romp in the wonderous stories that produced in me a variety of emotions. Each story brought new revelations for me. My second and third reading of the book was to focus on the stories that moved me most. I gave the book to my wife to read – she loved it too. Often, we would pick a story to read to each other and stories to read to our children. This book became a part of our lives.

I had already been a published writer and had, at the time that this book came into my life, been toying with the idea of experimenting with the short story form. This collection of wonderfully written short fiction spurred me on. I began to study the many different styles in the book. Now I was rereading the book with a critical eye. I was developing the fundamental critical formulas necessary for reading, understanding and judging what I read. I was also developing a feel for how the authors used certain elements, such as, conflict, argument, description, character, theme, symbolism and so on. I also picked up on many of the mechanisms individual authors invented to assist the readers of their work. In "The Old Man and the Sea, " Earnest Hemmingway describes in brilliant details, a location on the body of a whale where it had been harpooned. Then he immediately tells the readers that such a spot doesn't really exist, but insisted that now the reader know what he is talking about. All writers make up these inventions you don't learn about in a writing class or in a book about the writing of literature. This ability becomes possible once a writer has reached a certain level in proficiency and has found his or her writing voice. Plus, I don't believe that writers sit down and devise these devices, but rather, they come in a moment of inspiration.

Some years back, in the move from New York City to the Charleston, South Carolina area, that book came up missing. I had read it until the pages came loose – maybe it flew away. Now, of course, I'd like to think that I learned lots about writing short fiction from the writers contained in that anthology. And, that I've reached a level of expertise that I can reach outside of the textbook to invent my own literary mechanism when it becomes necessary. I'd also like to think that the stories in this book are brimming with examples of such inventiveness.

I've until now tried to convey how important my sister's high school English anthology was to my development as a writer of short fiction. However, it wasn't until I came across the stories of a writer named Isaac Bashevis Singer that I became aware that all of the special qualities embodied in say, ten, of the best writers in the anthology could all be embodied in one person. Singer, who wrote for the Daily Forward, wrote only in Hebrew so his otherwise published stories and novels had to be translated into English for American consumption and other languages around the world. Isaac Bashevis Singers moves through a story making me feel familiar with places, people, concepts and situations I had never known before – his story-telling is so natural. To read Singer is to be entertained by someone whose objective in not entertainment, but creation, and entertains just the same. Many of the stories in his collection "The Collected Stories of Isaac Bashevis Singer" takes place in pre war Poland and in post war New York City. Together they tell not only the story of the madness that was unleashed against the Jews, but binds all humanity together in a common universality.

Singer stories merged the casual with a sense of purpose, doubt that kindles faith. They are unique and general, realistic and mystical and they don't struggle with an obligation to explain themselves. Reading Singer gave me a higher goal to reach. I had to emulate Singer's originality and some how find my own voice.

A writer should only write about what he knows. In 1989 I with my wife, returned to South Carolina. I left in 1945, at the age of four, she in 1962 at the age of eighteen. I knew lots about the history of the South, but I didn't know a thing about the South – I hadn't enough experience with the South. So, when the idea came to me to write a collection of short stories fixed in the Charleston area, I had to get out and acquire a sense of the people and the customs. I had to get to know the back roads, the small towns and the cities. When I was satisfied that I had learned enough about the area and the people I had become apart of I started to write. None of the characters in the stories in this book, are real, rather, they are prototypes and imagination.

When I was a young boy, I used to spend the summer with my grandmother in what is now known as Hollywood, SC. Many days we would get short summer rains while the sun was still bright. I'd ask Momma Dolly why the sun was out when it was raining and her answer was always "The devil is beating his wife." What I think she was pointing out —is how good and evil can have the same appearance, inhibit the same domain, even live in the same person.

I spent almost as many years getting to know the subject of this collection as I did learning the craft of short fiction writing only to find that publishers don't take readily to the short fiction medium of story telling anymore. So, here, have a laugh with me; I have exhausted years trying to master a dying form – dying that is, unless you like what you will read here and tell your family and friends about it. And together we may be able to bring life back to the short fiction form.

It is said that the first Africans upon the slave ships headed to the America's sensed the coming of a great and lasting catastrophe. They knew that they needed something to protect and forify them from the coming cenuries of servitude and oppression, so they sent out an exalted wail beseeching God's mercy. God looked down on them and saw that they had nothing. they were naked and in chains. God, in His wisdom, took the very sound of their lamentation and turned it into their shield and their weapon and today we call that sound music. It is those majestic wails, that cry of despair, that music, in its ever-changing forms, that has nourished our people through the centuries.

Sleepy Willie

To Gussie, my wife, my music for 40 years.

THE MAN WHO HEARD THE DEAD

Dead people all have stories. Their stories, just as their aspirations and dreams, are often buried with them. The dead continue to exist, in the live realm, only in the fragile memories of the living, or by some prodigious contribution they made to society. Their stories; those little chunks of thought that roamed free in their heads every waking moment—are gone, not with them, but from them. In life, our aims, struggles, victories, and failures are the bones of our existence; the meat that cover and connect those bones are the events in our individual stories and these end with us and are believed to be forever irretrievable. "Hey everybody, lets have some fun—you only live but once and when you're dead, you're done. So let the good times roll."

I was driving back home from a visit with some cousins in Hollywood on a Saturday evening in March. My infrequent visits always involved the gathering of five or six cousins, some boiled crabs and shrimps, some good-natured teasing, lots of reminiscing, and several bottles of liquor—all under the familiar surrounding of a two hundred-year-old moss filled oak-tree. I live an hour's drive from the town where my mother and my father's family live—the town of my birth and youth. After college, I spent a few years teaching in Aiken. My first year there I met Josephine who was also a teacher in Aiken. We fell in love and after marriage, my wife and I settled in Beaufort where I teach in the Black Studies program at the junior college and she at the middle school. Highway 17 is an almost straight drive between Hollywood and Beaufort. Sometimes, after I've been drinking, I like to take what I call the scenic route; a group of secondary roads that blends and bends pleasingly through the woodland, swamps and several tiny rural communities. This route stretches out the drive back to Beaufort for another pleasant half an hour. I believe that there are more abandoned old country churches on this route than in any other part of the state of South Carolina. Most of these churches have small unkempt cemeteries that have been forsaken by their communities for fifty years, or longer, in some cases. As these communities grew or relocated, these old churches were replaced by larger modern structures more centrally located in the communities.

All of the churches are small weather beaten, wooden structures, with boarded up or missing windows and doors. The whitewash has turned brown and the wood is decayed. They were all, at one time, shining old-fashioned A-frame built houses of worship, whitewashed and well kept. When I drive by, I like to imagine them pristine. And, I like to imagine preachers delivering fire-and-brimstone sermons like those in James Weldon Johnson's book "God's Trombones." Sermons filled with the creative spirit of the old Negro preachers who captivated and uplifted the dispositions of burdened congregations throughout the South. Depending on how deep the fantasy pulls at me, I can sometimes picture the old cars, trucks and the hitched up horse drawn buggies in the churchyard. Then I imagine the congregation all dressed in their Sunday-going-to-meeting clothes, a spirited congregation of men, women, and children responding to the magnetism and power of a thunderously delivered sermon. Sometimes I can hear "Hallelujah" and "Amen," coming out from the walls of these churches. Once while driving by, I got so wrapped up in my imagined re-enactment of the scene in the church, that I joined in "hallelujah, hallelujah—preach preacher."

I feel so strongly about these old structures because I know the importance they played in uniting an impoverished and oppressed people, and making them feel that they belonged to something meaningful. These buildings were places where my people could release the heavy daily burdens of the world and feel the weightlessness of faith. Places where they could beseech God's mercy and gain hope. These old churches were the palaces built with the pennies of the destitute and are themselves monuments to the communal faith of people who held God close to their bosom—our ancient ruins. And, I feel strongly about those old-time country preachers who led the flocks. These were men of great vision and resilience, who were themselves, most often, farmers, carpenters and common laborers during the week, but on Sundays they were shepherds delivering messages directly from God. I once heard a preacher preach, "You can't buy your way into the Kingdom, no matter how much money you've got. The currency of salvation is faith." These old churches are testimony to the wealth of a people. My drive down this road gives me a chance to visit with an era gone by and an opportunity to be reminded of the durability of my people. I like to smile my tribute to them.

It had just recently turned dark. I was approaching the last abandoned church on this stretch of road when my headlights caught a figure over to the far end of the church. As I was about to pass, the figure appeared to collapse to the ground in the graveyard. I stopped driving, backed the car up and parked it, but left it running by the side of the road. I got out of the car cautiously. I walked to the graveyard and found a man lying, face down, alongside a grave marked by an old gray stone.

"Are you alright buddy?" I asked. The man said nothing. I moved in closer.

"Hey, mister, are you alright?" I said louder. "Hey, do you need any help?" Still, there was no answer. I moved in even closer and was about to touch him when he turned to look up at me. He was a light-skinned man a little older than I was, but still under forty. He had a pleasant face that looked familiar although I had never seen him before.

"I'm alright. I don't need any help. Go ahead now. Thank you."

"What are you doing lying there?"

"I don't need no help—you wouldn't understand. Gone now."

"Look, my car is right there and still running. I can take you to the hospital in town—you need a doctor—of some kind," I said somewhat derisively.

"My car is on the other side of the church," the man said softly. "I said I don't need your help. Now please leave me."

The man didn't sound to be distraught or suicidal, so although I was mystified, I reluctantly returned to my car and drove off. I didn't know what to make of this guy and I couldn't get him out of my head. When I got home, I told Josephine about the incident. "You want something to eat?" she asked, walking to the kitchen. Her tone suggested she thought I had had too much to drink. A few years back, I told her about how I would imagine seeing and hearing the old congregations at those old abandoned churches, but I made it clear to her that it was just a creative exercise to pass time. She thought it a bit strange and even spooky. Now, I was fearful she was thinking that the whiskey made me take this fantasy too far. We ate dinner, watched a little television and went to bed without me ever mentioning the event again.

The weather in March of 2002 was continually uncertain—it rained most of the month and the temperature was unseasonably cold. I caught a pretty bad cold that kept me from work for an entire week. Josephine's family lives in Beaufort and on the third day that I was laid up in bed, her Aunt Cora came to pay a visit. Aunt Cora evaluated my condition and told Josephine to go to the herbal shop to get me some ginger tea. The next morning, Josephine said that she would stop after school to get the ginger tea. I told her that I needed to get out of the house. I got directions to the shop from her and made the drive myself.

I was surprised that I had never noticed the shop before. It is located on an attractive side street of stylish shops, downtown in the historic district. It has an engaging wooden sign with the words "The Healing Den," burned onto it. I went into the shop. The pungent aromas of all kinds of medicinal herbs immediately assaulted my nostrils. The herbs were in open wooden barrels and marked with signs that stuck out from the barrels. There were metal tree stands scattered about with clamps that held bags of powders, twigs, leaves and barks. Over to the right were shelves of books on herbal healing and raw vegetable juices. The counter held a huge juice extractor and next to it was a plastic tub of carrots, apples, celery, heads of lettuce and cabbage and roots that I later found out were ginger and cinnamon. The vegetables in the tub were topped with a layer of chipped ice. There were African artifacts spread about the store. Two plastic tables with chairs sat over to the left of the counter and provided a view of the street out through the store window. Also on the counter were flyers with printed menus of herbal remedies to treat this or that ailment. Brightly colored kente cloth curtains covered the doorway that led to the storeroom behind the counter.

I had time to really look the place over before I saw a hand pulling the curtains aside and a figure finally emerged. I recognized him instantly. It was the light-skinned fellow I saw that Saturday evening lying in the graveyard. "Good morning, what can I offer you this lovely morning," he said pleasantly, apparently not remembering my face.

"Good morning," I said, somewhat uncomfortably.

"You want some time to look around?" he asked.

"No—I have a cold. My wife's Aunt Cora recommended some ginger tea."

"Do you want bagged ginger tea or loose ginger tea?"

"I don't know, but let me tell you, I come downtown fairly often and I've never seen this place before. How long have you been here? Oh, I'm sorry—my name is Joshua Brown."

"I'm Lee Jordan," he said, extending his hand. "The shop has been here for five years. Now, do you own a glass teapot?"

"A glass teapot—I don't think so?"

"Then you'll want the bagged ginger tea. I have two commercial brands that come twenty in a box and I have bags that I make up myself. I also have loose ginger roots."

"You don't remember me?"

"We've met?"

"I'm the fellow who saw you lying in the graveyard in that old abandoned church on Route 15 a couple of Saturdays ago. That was you, wasn't it?"

"Yeah."

"You know—I like to drive that route to see those old churches. I think that those old buildings are as revealing a part of our history as anything written. Here is something I've only told my wife. When I drive down 15, I like to visualize the old people in those churches and even hear them singing those old spirituals. I'm really fond of those old churches, but,

I'm thinking that you may have an even greater affection for them"

"That's interesting. Do you have a cough with your cold?"

"No, I just feel like ten miles of bad road."

"I'll boil up some loose ginger for you while you make up your mind which form of ginger you want and maybe we'll talk a little." Lee went to a barrel marked with a ginger sign. He put some leaves in a paper bag and took it back behind the curtains.

I'm certain I found it easy to disclose my peculiarity to him because of what I viewed as his own strangeness. And, the ease of my self-disclosure seemed to open him up with the offering of a cup of tea. I was expecting that with the hot ginger tea would come some transparency on his part. I was really interested in knowing why he laid on the ground in the graveyard, yet I was apprehensive about what he would say. I could hear the water running and the commotion he made preparing the tea.

"Would you like a teaspoon of honey in your tea?" he asked.

"Yes, thank you. That would be fine."

In a few minutes, Lee returned with two steaming cups of tea. He took them over to a table and gestured for me to sit down.

"This tea is stronger than the commercial ones I sell. You have to prepare it in a glass pot and you have to strain it—but it's a much better product for the treatment of a cold."

"Oh, it is," I said.

"What do you do for a living?"

"I'm a teacher. I teach Black History at the junior college. My wife is from this area. I taught at a college in Aiken for a few years. Then three years ago, this opportunity came along. My wife is also a teacher—she teaches science at the middle school. Man, she's happy to be back home and I don't mind it here. I'm from Hollywood, but I find this to be a very lovely area."

I looked at the tea. It was a pale brown color with a hint of green. I took a sip. It was too hot—I blew into it and sat the cup down.

"My folks were born and raised here," Lee said, "but they moved to Baltimore in the early sixties. That's where I was born in 1964. I graduated from the University of Maryland with a degree in Cultural Anthropology."

"Cultural Anthropology that puts you in the history business too—doesn't it?"

"You can say that. I wanted to follow the work of Zora Neal Hurston and write a definitive work on the cultural evolution of black Americans from day one of slavery to now."

"Wow," I said. "Are you still at work on that? Sounds like a life-long project to me. I know that there are several branches of anthropology and I would think that cultural anthropology is the study of human cultural developments and traditions. Archeologists are the ones concerned with graves. Right?"

"I'm doing some pioneer work," Lee said sipping from his tea now that it had cooled. "As you've said, there are several branches of anthropology, I'm pioneering in a new branch."

"A new branch of anthropology that makes you lie on graves?"

"I'm developing something I call Spiritual Anthropology— the study and collection of the stories of the dead, from the dead."

I took too large a sip from my teacup and had to cough some of it up. I reached for my handkerchief and wiped myself off.

"I'm sorry," I said.

"It must have been something I said. Your tea should have cooled off some by now.

"Stories from the dead?" I asked.

"Yeah, would you like to hear about my experience so far—do you have time?"

I took another sip of tea and forgot all about my cold.

I spent the rest of the morning and half of the afternoon talking and listening to Lee, in between customers. Lee is a soft-spoken man with a tremendously convincing manner. He's got this way of really pulling you into whatever he's saying. His father and mother both worked while he was growing up in Baltimore. His mother was a nurse and his father joined the Baltimore police department and rose through the ranks to become the first black captain in the homicide division. Lee was an only child and was showered with everything, but especially an appreciation for education. He went to private grade school in Baltimore, which prepared him well for anything he wanted to study at the University of Maryland. Lee had seen much of the world. His family vacationed abroad every year. He had been to countries in Europe, Africa, South America and the Caribbean. Lee's parents moved back to Beaufort after they were both retired and in a few years, Lee followed.

He never worked in his field of study. After college, he floated around between New York, Chicago, Atlanta, San Francisco and back to Baltimore working at odd jobs. In New York, he worked for the city's Child Welfare Department. In Chicago, he worked for an anthropology publication. In San Francisco, he waited tables at a popular restaurant in the Bay area. In Atlanta, he opened a small bookshop. Lee loved books and he loved to read. When he returned to Baltimore, he opened another bookshop. He started using herbs and learning all he could about them. When he became comfortable with his knowledge on herbs, he began to sell them in his bookshop. When he moved to Beaufort, he stopped selling general books and opened the Healing Den. The only books he carried now were ones on herbs and raw vegetable juices. Lee never made many friends and he never married. He had very little interest in a serious relationship at this point in his life. He was presently seeing a woman who owned the African artifact shop across the street from his shop.

Lee's interest turned to Spiritual Anthropology two years ago when his father died. He was dedicated to his parents; he loved them both dearly. His father's death ate at him for months, then something strange happened. His father came to him in a dream and told him to visit his grave. His father is buried in the modern well-kept cemetery at Wesley Baptist Church on the eastside of Beaufort. He was so happy for the dream that when he got up that morning he went straight to his father's grave at the cemetery. Nothing happened, but he was so sure of his father's message that he didn't despair. He visited the grave at different times of the day and evenings for a month. Then, one night, despondency sat upon him and he threw himself down on his father's grave and blacked out. While he was out, he had a clairvoyant experience. When he came around there was no memory of the experience, only a dry mouth and a strong feeling that he had made contact with his father. Lee was sure his father told him something. He was positive that he had gone through an extrasensory experience, but he had no memory of it and trying to remember it, only made the feeling more obscure.

Lee was so confident of his feelings of having made contact with his father, that one morning he told his mother about the dream and his experience at the grave. He asked her if she knew what it all meant. Nora Jordan, a light-skinned woman of great dignity and forbearance, showed no surprise at her son's question. "People say your grandfather was second-sighted and could hear from beyond. They said the same thing about your grandfather's grandfather," Lee's mother told him. She explained that it was something that occurred in his father's family almost every other generation like a bouncing gene that lay dormant for twenty years—then reappeared. "I don't know son, but maybe that's what your dad told you." She said enough to persuade Lee to believe that he had inherited his family's telepathic DNA without saying it outright.

At this point, I found Lee Jordan to be a very interesting person. Eccentric maybe, but he wasn't crazy. It even occurred to me that he might be at that thin line between the two—where genius resides. He reminded me of a guy I once knew in college. A chess player, who wondered everyday, whether every series of moves in every chess match ever played by novice or expert players, had already been played. If this was true, he would say beaming, as if he had discovered a principle as important as Einstein's theory of relativity, then every chess game played today is a redundancy. This question was a burning part of his life. He bored us all to sleep with this question, but no one at our school could beat him at chess, or beat him in a debate. This guy was absolutely in that zone. I heard a few years back that he had become one of the nation's top black Republicans and that he writes position papers for a conservative think tank in Washington D.C. that advises the president on foreign policy. Before I left Lee that day, I told him that I would call back to invite him to dinner after I had cleared the date with Josephine.

That evening Josephine and I had a very interesting conversation during dinner. I told her about finding the guy

I saw lying on the ground in the graveyard several weeks past and that he is the owner of the herb shop. I told her all about our conversation, particularly his pioneering experiments and Lee's mother's affirmation of his divination. She was bewildered, but interested in meeting Lee. In a few days, I was fit again and back to my regular routine. Josephine and I agreed that I would invite Lee over for the coming Saturday evening. I called Lee, he seemed happy to hear from me. He accepted our invitation and asked if he could bring Sandy Adams, the owner of the African artifact shop, with him. I told him I looked forward to seeing them on Saturday evening.

They arrived at seven and our evening began with the first surprise. Sandy Adams was a white woman, friendly and intelligent, but her appearance made us self-conscious of the fact that we automatically expected a black woman. Sandy is a pleasant woman, about, I'd say, 33—my age. She is a pretty woman with dark hair and bright blue eyes. Our surprise went unnoticed and we quickly adjusted our thinking. Sandy brought a bottle of wine and Lee a bag of three different herbs. After we all got introduced, Josephine brought out a vegetable platter and we all settled down with a conversation that first centered on Sandy. She told us that after apartheid was over in South Africa, she lived there for two years. It was there that she fell in love with African art. She knew right off that, for her, it would never be satisfying enough just to be a collector, she had to acquire large stocks of carvings, masks, instruments, paintings, beadwork, religious icons and everything else she could lay her hands on to expose people back home to these magnificent works. She returned back to Beaufort, and found the perfect shop for her business on Spring Street. She named her shop The Trading Post. Once a year, she goes back to Cape Town to purchase stock and renew old contacts.

What I had learned of Lee's life-style made me suspect that he might be on a modified diet, but I was thinking maybe just no pork or red meat. So, for the night's dinner, we planned to serve grilled chicken beast, a three-bean salad and wild rice. I had no idea that he had gone all the way. He was a strict vegetarian. Sandy was a vegetarian who eats some fish, turkey, and mercifully, some chicken. I opened a bottle of my own wine while the one Sandy brought chilled, only to find out that Lee didn't drink. Josephine boiled him some mint tea. After Josephine and I talked a little about our teaching experiences, Lee introduced his subject. We all sipped wine and listened as he told us what his mother had told him about his family's history with telepathic clairvoyance. The rumor had been passed down through his family, that near the end of slavery, his great, great grandfather conducted channeling sessions to get people in touch with their love ones in the beyond. His grandfather did the same during the depression. Lee told us that he suspected that he received this gift through his genetic makeup and that he was anxious to have it affirmed by a witness.

Josephine set the table and we sat for dinner. Lee said that he would have the three-bean salad and an extra serving of rice. During dinner, Lee asked me if I would accompany him when he went out again. He wanted me to witness whatever occurred, since he would have no memory of it and he wanted me to record whatever was said so he would have a proof of it. Josephine looked a little put-off by the topic of the dinner conversation, and she smiled at me to let me know. Lee said he was eager to apply the knowledge he gained in anthropology at the University of Maryland to this experience and to have it all chronicled. He envisioned writing a study that he could turn into a book. I looked at Josephine. She looked at Sandy and asked her if she wanted another glass of wine? This was her way of telling me that this was my decision to make. As Sandy poured wine in her glass, I asked Lee if he would like another cup of tea. He said he did and Josephine went to the kitchen to make the tea. While she was gone, I agree to accompany Lee.

When Josephine returned we all went into the den to listen to music and chat. I played some blues and Motown discs from the seventies. Lee asked if I had any fifties and sixties' jazz. I confessed that I didn't have any jazz of any period. I told Josephine of my decision and she smiled a half smile. All the time my music played, Lee explained the esthetics of mid twentieth century jazz. Lee talked about Miles Davis, Thelonious Monk, John Coltrane and he told us some amusing stories about the tragic life of Charlie Parker. Lee was very knowledgeable about the history of jazz and he had a way of talking about it that made it interesting. By the time they left, I was determined to buy some jazz music.

On Sunday evening, Lee called to ask if I would meet him on Wednesday evening at seven o'clock. He would be at the same church where I first saw him. I agreed and asked if I should bring my old tape recorder. He said that he had purchased a new one that would be more suitable to our purpose. It was digital and weatherproof. After the phone call, I told Josephine that I would meet Lee on Wednesday evening. She reacted in a way that suggested that she had become intrigued by the project. "I want to know all about it," she said in an enthusiastic voice filled with anticipation.

When I arrived at the church, I saw Lee's car parked where it was parked the Saturday evening that I first met him. I parked my car next to his. Lee was over in the graveyard. We greeted each other and he gave me the small digital recorder. He explained how it operated and I ran through a couple of trial runs to be sure that I understood how it worked. Lee showed me the grave he had selected. The headstone was that of a young girl named Sarah Breland, born 1950—died 1959. Lee asked if I was ready. I said that I was, although I had a strange feeling in my stomach. Lee said some kind of exotic prayer and threw himself on the grave embracing it. I knelt down near him with the recorder near his face. I had the recorder set so that I just needed to press the record button at the first sound that came from him. I took a deep silent breath as doubt started to set in on me. Three minutes went by with nothing happening. I changed my position a little to be more comfortable. Lee's face began to move back and forth, slowly at first, then it moved violently. I pressed the record button, but there was no sound. I pressed the stop button and just then, a girl's voice moaned out:

"No daddy. Daddy please—no daddy. Daddy I don't want to do that. Daddy why you always make me do that. Daddy, momma don't want me to do that. Daddy please don't hit me. I ain't gonna tell momma. Daddy please don't hit me 'gain. I ain't gonna tell nobody –but, daddy please don't make me do this no mo'—please daddy."

The voice had a tremor and pitch of a frightened young girl, but something in me allowed for the likelihood that Lee was faking this whole thing. In the seconds of silence between the last word and the time Lee's face stopped moving, my mind raced through the possibility that Lee could be using me to validate a cruel hoax. Lee continued to lie silently. Three minutes elapsed before Lee could move. Then he rose up. He looked tired and worn; his face had a gentle twist to it.

"I've got it," I said, somewhat skeptical.

"How much? Did she speak?" he asked, as his face transformed back to normal right in front of my eyes.

"About a minute," I said. " It was the girl, I think. Do you remember anything? We might have a minute of her story here on the recorder. Do you want to hear it?"

"No. No, not now. I'll take it back with me. I feel like I need to prepare myself to hear this. I don't think I could take it right now. I'll call you tomorrow."

I gave the recorder to Lee. We walked back to our cars, shook hands and drove off. I drove home feeling more doubtful than ever. I didn't really know the guy. I wondered why he didn't want to hear the recorder in my presence. He took anthropology in college—that's not a popular field, especially for a black student. Could he also have taken some acting lessons?

At home, I told Josephine everything that transpired. I believe I recalled the séance word for word. I told Josephine about the voice of an abused girl-child and the distortion of Lee's face. I told her that although it seemed real, I had my doubts.

"Joshua, what was the girl's name?"

"Sarah Breland."

"Call Aunt Cora and ask her if she knows any Brelands."

I picked up the telephone and dialed Aunt Cora's number. Josephine sat in a chair next to me so she could monitor the conversation.

"Hello," Aunt Cora answered, after the third ring.

"Good evening Aunt Cora, this is Joshua. How are you?"

"Boy, don't you think I know your voice by now. I'm doing well. How are you and my sweet niece?"

"We've fine. Josephine's right here—she suggested that I call you to ask you something."

"And what is that?"

"I want to know if you know any people with the last name of Breland?"

"Breland—they used to be a large family of Brelands that lived out there on Highway 15, cross the creek in Lobeco. 15 was just a dirt road back then. They worked on the farm of Mr. Sam Taylor. I don't know whatever became of those people. No farming done out there for years and years now."

"Aunt Cora, did any of them have a daughter named Sarah?"

"I can't say that I know that. I do remember that one of them had a young child that was found drowned in the creek between Beaufort and Lobeco—Lord that was a long time ago. Yes, I believe that was sometime back in the 60's."

"Could it have been in 1959?"

"It could have been. I only remember that it was a long time ago."

"Was it a boy or girl?"

"Now I do remember that. It was a little girl. I remember there was all kinds of talk about it. Some folks said that the child had drowned herself, but I never put much stock in that. What could make an innocent little child do that to herself? Some folk said that some of them mean old Kluxer's did it, but near as I can tell, the truth was never to be found."

"Thank you Aunt Cora. You're a doll."

"Now what's this all about?"

"Nothing much—Aunt Cora, I know Josephine told you about my affection for those old churches on 15. Well, I saw the headstone for that little girl and wondered about it. Aunt Cora, Josephine says love and kisses and I'll talk to you soon. Now you have a good night. Bye-bye."

"Did you hear that?" I asked Josephine. "Did you hear that? A girl did drown. Aunt Cora isn't sure of the year or the name, but the event did happen and Lee's got the reason why on his recorder."

"Don't you think you'll need some collaboration before you form a solid opinion?" Josephine asked.

"Yeah, you're right. Tomorrow after classes, I'll get Lee and drive out to Lobeco to see if any of those people still live out there."

I was preparing my classes for a test at the end of the month. The test was on the period of the civil rights movement I call: Rosa Parks to Memphis. Today's lesson covered the reasons Dr. King went to Memphis. I had planned a dramatic summation of all the factors leading up to Dr. King's assassination, but that little girl's anguish pulled at me all day and I gave a less than effectual classroom performance. After my last class, I drove to Lee's shop on Spring Street.

"I was going to call you this evening," Lee said as I entered the shop.

"I've got some news for you," I said.

"I could hardly believe my ears when I played the recorder. That voice came out of my mouth—she spoke through me. This is fantastic, unbelievable, and supernatural. Sarah Breland told her story through me."

"And, I think I can confirm it. A young girl was found drowned in the creek out there around the time of Sarah's death."

"How do you know that?" Lee asked.

"I called Josephine's Aunt Cora, the one who told me about the ginger tea. She told me about the Brelands. They lived and worked on a farm in Lobeco. The girl was found drowned, but it was never clear, how it happened."

"Ah, but we know what happened. We know what her father did to her. Her own father drove her to it"

"You think she killed herself?"

"You heard her anguish."

"Yeah, but what if the father did it to keep her from talking. I figure a man that did what we suspect he did to his own daughter would be capable of anything. I came by so we could go out to Lobeco to find out what there is to learn."

"We'll get to that," Lee said. "I'd like to approach this by collecting all the stories we can, then investigate and collaborate them one by one. I don't know the extent of my abilities, so while it's working collect, collect, collect—then investigate, investigate, investigate."

Lee's plan seemed reasonable to me. He was the one with the gift and he was the one with an education in the principles of anthropology –although I didn't quite know which field what we were doing fit into.

"When do you want to go out again," I asked.

"I'll call you. I need to go out to get a feel for which one will be our next study. Then I'll call you in a day or two."

I left for home feeling disappointed. Deep down, I felt we should have gone out to Lobeco to find out whatever we could. If there was any validity to what we thought we knew, then we also had a responsibility to Sarah to seek justice. I considered going out to Lobeco to ask some questions that would bring answers that would refute or confirm our suspicion. I didn't dismiss the idea completely, but then something else came into my mind. I was also disappointed about my sub-standard performance in my classroom. I thought about tomorrow and how I would have to spend more time on my lessons on the Memphis sanitation worker's impasse and the injustices and disparities the presence of Dr. King was to bring focus too. I would also bring my old tape recorder to play Dr. King's last speech in which he talked about the threats that were made on his life after his arrival in Memphis.

When I told Josephine about the situation, she agreed with my opinion that we had an obligation to find out what happened to little Sarah and to seek some degree of justice for her. She even offered to go to Lobeco with me. Josephine got the telephone book. Lobeco is in Beaufort County and its phone listings, as are all the other small towns in the county, are listed in the Beaufort telephone book. There were eight Brelands listed for Lobeco in the book. Josephine wrote the names, addresses, and numbers on a sheet of paper and gave it to me. I gathered up my tape recorder, a note pad and pen. I told Josephine that I would be back in a couple of hours and went out of the house feeling like I was doing the right thing.

The first two homes I visited were occupied by people in their early thirties. In both cases, it was the male of the household who was a Breland descendant. None of them had ever heard of Sarah Breland, who would have been 52 years old had she lived, and might have been a grand aunt or third cousin to them. The people in the next house were in their 50's and what they knew about Sarah and the incident was hazy. They directed me to an older uncle who lived by himself. His name was Arthur Breland and he looked to be around 80 years old.

I introduced myself to the old man as a teacher of Negro history. I told him that I was researching information on the family of the little girl who drowned here in 1959. Arthur Breland spoke freely. He told me that he was Otis Breland's first cousin. Otis Breland is Sarah's father. Otis Breland's wife was named Suzy and they had six children, two boys and four girls. Sarah was the youngest child. Arthur described Sarah as a troubled child whose behavior was odd. She seemed to fear her father and would tremble in his presence. Sarah never looked anyone in the eyes. She always steered away from anyone who spoke to her. There was something wrong with Sarah, Arthur asserted, but he never could figure out what it was. He was surprised as everyone else, when they found Sarah's body in the creek. He remembered the day. He and his brother Charles, Otis and his brother Frank, had all been in the field picking cotton from a little before sun-up until a little after sundown. They arrived back home that night tired and hungry and wanted nothing more than to eat and to rest. There were six Breland households in a section still today called "The Quarters." They each went home to a household full of grief. Two months after he buried his daughter, Otis Breland took his family to Tennessee to work the season and, most people thought, to get away from the rumors.

I now knew that Otis Breland did not physically kill his daughter. I wanted to ask Arthur Breland, if Otis had been known to sexually molest Sarah, but I couldn't find a way to ask such a delicate question. All the while he talked, I searched my mind for an appropriate approach to the question. Then, Arthur told me something that made my question unnecessary. It seems that a month after the family settled down on a tenant farm in Tennessee, Otis Breland was found in bed with the wife of a fellow tenant farmer. The husband came home from the fields unexpectedly and saw the two of them through a window. His loaded shotgun hung over the door and if he went, right then, into the one room shack, there might have been a struggle for the gun. The husband returned to the fields unseen by the lovers. The next day, right after lunchtime, gunshots could be heard in all the connecting fields of the farm. Most people didn't pay much attention to the gunshots thinking someone may have killed a snake. The people closest to the noise of the gun went to see what they thought would have been a snake, but instead, they found Otis

Breland shot to death, his head nearly blown off. And that was that, Arthur Breland said. There was no investigating, no charges, no arrest—just an unceremonious burial with no tears. Sarah had received a degree of justice without any further smearing of her name.

I shared all of this with Josephine and we agreed that it would be best if I held what I found out, away from Lee, at least for now. I taped everyone I talked with and I took notes of the conversation with Arthur Breland. In my notes, I recorded the inflections that a tape recorder cannot capture, like the ease with which Arthur spoke or my impression that something besides my questions had brought these ancient memories so readily to his mind.

The next morning, Lee called before I left the house for work. He wanted me to meet him at a church a mile down the road from the church where Sarah is buried. He told me that he had plugged the digital recorder into his computer and transferred Sarah's voice onto a diskette. Then he deleted the voice from the recorder to ensure that we had maximum space. He asked me to be there at the same time as before. During classes that day, I found myself at peace with poor Sarah's situation and I was able to concentrate on the material I was offering to my students.

A few minutes before I arrived at the church, rain began to fall lightly. This church was off from the road a good bit and the roadway into its yard was overgrown with grass and weeds. Lee had parked his car on the shoulder of Highway 15. I parked behind his car, making sure that my car was completely off of the road. I saw Lee standing in the graveyard. He had his hand on the headstone of the grave that would be his subject this evening. I had once again grown suspicious of Lee. I no longer considered his gift fraudulent; my suspicion was less tangible.

His not wanting to investigate the conditions of Sarah's death sparked my distrust for Lee. I waved without saying anything until I was close enough to shake hands.

"Hey Joshua," Lee said, letting my hand go and returning his hand to the headstone. "How are you this evening?"

"I'm fine. How are you?"

"Man, I've been listening to Sarah's voice over and over again. I'm becoming obsessed with it—I'm so fired up about this discovery. I've been thinking about the book, you know, kind of laying out the format and outline."

I looked at the name on the headstone. This was the grave of another rather young person: Solomon James, born 1942, died 1960. I didn't reply to Lee's last comment. He seemed fixated on the book part of this whole experiment. He gave me a quizzical look.

"We better get started before the rain gets harder," I said.

"Good idea," Lee handed me the recorder and we went over its operation once again. Lee repeated the prayer he said at Sarah's grave. He turned to the grave and just as before, he fell to it and embraced it. I knelt down next to him with the recorder ready to go. In a minute, Lee began to growl. It was a human growl, like clearing the throat of a fish bone. I cut the recorder on although for a full minute, there was no other sound but the growl. Then:

"Solomon, you can't get away with this—it won't work boy. I don't know what done got into your mind—but you know damm well you can't kill a white man and get off. Boy I tell you what—you put that money back and I'll forget all about it —but you can't work for me no mo'. I can't have a stealing nigger like you in my store. Ooouch. Nigger, you shot me. You shot me! Now Solomon, I never treated you like the way I did all the other niggers and you know that."

This was supposed to be the grave of an 18-year-old black boy. The voice that came from Lee's mouth sounded southern and male, but elderly and white. The voice changed and now I could hear the agony of a man in pain. The rain started to fall more intensely. I could hear the rumbling of distant thunder in the sky.

"They gonna hang you when they find you out. Everybody in the county knows that I got that money for selling that track of land on Hilton Head. You been working 'round here—off and on, for five years—they gonna come for you. They gonna hang your black ass. Solomon put that gas can down—please. Come on boy, I was gonna run off with that money anyhow. I was gonna run off to Memphis and live it up. Now you help me up and I'll take you with me. There's plenty 'nough for you and me. Put that gas can down and we'll go to Memphis."

There was another shriek and then muffled screams—then blurry words. I couldn't see Lee's face, but I imagine it distorted with agony. There was the sound of heavy breathing that grew faint and then silent. I turned the recorder off. Lee laid there as he had been, and then he curled up in a fetal position and shook. I stood up and walked the kinks out of my knees. Lee laid there for three more minutes, then he rose up slowly. He was rubbing his folded arms from the shoulders to the elbows. The rain fell from his face.

"Are you alright Lee?" I asked. Lee looked dazed. His eyes were rolled back and appeared all white. He stopped rubbing his arms to touch his legs.

"Are you alright?" I repeated.

"I—feel—like—I—was on fire," Lee said, his voice was dry and hoarse.

I took Lee by his arms and led him to his car and out of the rain. I put him in the front passenger seat and I sat behind him with the digital recorder in my hand.

"That wasn't Solomon who spoke." I said. "You've got to hear this and I mean right now."

"I don't know if I can."

"Did you hear me? That was supposed to be the grave of Solomon James. The person who spoke was confronting Solomon. There was some kind of violence happening."

I pushed the play button. The recorder started with the last three growls before the person spoke. Lee looked down to his feet, but he listened as the whole thing replayed. When it ended, he looked at me in amazement.

"We just recorded what could have been a murder," he said.

"You damn right. We've got to take this to the sheriff."

"Don't be a fool," Lee said. "Nobody's going to believe that such a thing is possible. Look, let me handle this—I'm an anthropologist, I've got to document and authenticate my findings. There is a procedure for this process. I need to collect all my raw data, investigate and analyze that data then put it in order for the writing of my paper. I asked you to help me because I was sure that you would not interfere with how I managed the process."

Right then, I knew that I wouldn't tell Lee what I found out about Sarah. I also knew that I would try to find out what I could about Solomon James.

"So you're going to sit on information about a possible murder?"

"Look, Joshua, if there was a murder, it happened more than forty-two years ago. If no one has solved it in all that time, another year or so isn't going to change anything."

"A year?" I shouted.

"Yeah," Lee said. "I should have a paper ready in about a year. Then I'll spring it on the authorities; the publicity will be helpful to the publication of my paper and hopefully get a major publisher interested in it for a book. That's my plan."

"Okay, you're running the show," I said, getting out of the car. I took two steps towards my own car parked behind Lee's car. As I reached for the door, Lee asked for the recorder. I thought about resisting for a moment, but I handed him the recorder. "I guess I'll be hearing from you," I said without waiting for an answer. Lee said something, but by then, I was in my car pulling off.

When I got home, I had cooled off some and spoke calmly about what took place when Josephine asked me. I looked in the telephone book for people with James as their last name. The James's were spread out with a few in many different towns, but the bulk appeared in the town of Delk, which is on the other side of Lobeco. This is where I would start my search. Josephine suggested we spend the coming weekend in Savannah to get away from it all. Josephine is a thoughtful and caring wife—and a lovely woman. I could tell from the look on her face, that she was genuinely concerned for me and was trying to change my frame of mind. I love Savannah –the grand old churches, the parks, the art galleries and the restaurants on Rivers Avenue. I kissed Josephine and said, sure, Savannah for the weekend.

After classes the next day, I drove out to Delk. I selected the first name on my list: Mrs. Bertha James, 110 James Road. Delk has a main street with a gas station and Food Mart, a feed and seed store, a barbecue restaurant, an old-time general store, a juke-joint and a blinking caution light by the town's municipal building. I found James Road about three miles down from Main Street. Three hundred feet of dirt road led to 110. A black mailbox with white painted numbers is nailed to a wooden post imbedded in the ground. 110 is a small wooden house, with a metal fence around it. I parked my car near the mailbox. As I made my way to the door, I could hear dragging footsteps. The door opened before I knocked. An old woman stood at the door with inquiring eyes. I asked if she was Mrs. Bertha James. She nodded yes. I introduced myself and asked if I could come in. she opened the door wider and pointed to a chair for me to be seated. Her gray hair was in one big braid. Her skin was clear and healthy looking. Her eyes were big and watery.

"I wonder if I can ask you some questions about the death of Solomon James," I said, assuming that she was related to Solomon and that she knew something about his situation.

"What you wanna know," she answered in a high-pitch voice.

"Are you related to Solomon?"

"His daddy was my youngest brother. My daddy had nine head of children. I am the oldest and the only one still living. All my brothers and sisters got married off. I never married— reckon that's why I'm still alive?"

"What can you tell me about Solomon?"

"I guess you want to hear the story too."

"The story? Yes I'd like to hear the story."

"Solomon used to work for a peckerwood named Ed Moultrie, who had a little old grocery store here in the colored section. Mr. Moultrie had his house way on the other side of Delk, but he made his living selling goods to coloreds, mostly on credit. Anybody old enough to remember would tell you that Ed Moultrie was a mean thieving peckerwood. He charged us double what it was worth and you was gonna pay him or pay God. That son-of-a-gun, once shot a 12 year old boy in his hand over a piece of candy. That was a mean man, you hear me. Well, he wasn't mean to Solomon. I never known why—it must be 'cause he needed somebody to watch after his store when he gone home. Ever since Solomon was 13 years old, he would help out 'round the store, cleaning and toting things. Some children broke into the store one evening. I don't believe they took a thing. They was too 'fraid. After that, Mr. Moultrie set out a cot in the back room for Solomon to sleep on. Showed him where he kept his pistol and how to use it. He told Solomon to shoot anybody that broke into his store and not to worry 'bout it—there wouldn't be no trouble."

"Anyway, Mr. Moultrie owned some land somewhere up there in Hilton Head. They say that he sold the land to some people who was building them big old homes you see on Hilton Head. That was back in 1960, Solomon been working for Mr. Moultrie for five years and just turned 18 years old. Even 'fore that peckerwood got the money, he been telling people that he was gonna run off to Memphis and leave his wife and her mamma who lived with them. That man been in his late fifties and was bragging 'bout what he was gonna do to them young hens in Memphis. He talk so much 'bout it that everybody known that he got fifty thousand dollars for the land. That's enough money to live like a millionaire, he used to say."

"Solomon always had to be off to his self. The other colored children didn't like him and talked nasty 'bout him. He caught a tough time in school too, but they didn't beat him 'fraid for what Mr. Moultrie would do back. I guess Solomon figured he done give up a lot for that white man against his own people. Solomon known that Mr. Moultrie hide the money in a metal box in the back of the store waiting for the day he would run off to Memphis. One night, after they closed the store, Solomon came down on Mr. Moultrie's head with a piece of two by four—knocked him clean out. Solomon picked Mr. Moultrie up and carried him to my brother's house, which wasn't too far behind the store. Solomon tied him good to a chair and stuff cloth in his mouth and put taped 'round that. My brother, his wife and the other two children had gone to Atlanta for a week, so they didn't know a thing 'bout this—at the time."

"Well, Solomon let two days past without the store opening up for business. He told everybody he seed, colored or white, that Mr. Moultrie musta run off to Memphis like he promise to do. On the evening of the second day, he went to see Mr. Moultrie's wife to ask her 'bout him and to tell her that the store been closed for two days. He told her that he was still sleeping in the store to guard against thievery and fire. Before he left he told Mrs. Moultrie that he often heard Mr. Moultrie talking about going off to Memphis and the last thing he said to her in his politest colored voice was 'You reckon.' That evening Solomon took Mr. Moultrie back to the store and let him watch as he took the metal box with the money from its hiding place. He shot Mr. Moultrie a few times with him pleading for his life, then he took two full gas cans and poured gas all over the man and his store. Solomon took the old iron bracelet he wore all the time and put it on Mr. Moultrie's *wrist.* He opened the back door, struck a match and threw it into the store. Solomon went home, picked up a few things and unseen he left town that night. People saw the store on fire, but nobody thought to go put it out. And the next day, when the fire was cooled enough to get near, they found a body burned so bad you couldn't make out who it was, but Solomon's bracelet was on its wrist."

"When my brother and his family returned from Atlanta, we buried Solomon in the cemetery of Mount Olive Baptist church on Highway 15."

"Only it wasn't Solomon who was buried," I said.

"No, it wasn't," Mrs. James kind of smiled. "We didn't know it at the time and my brother went to his grave not knowing the truth. It wasn't until 1980, when my brother died that some of us found out the truth. Solomon came home for his father's funeral. He told a few of us older ones how he killed that man, took his money and went off to Chicago. Solomon is a big business man in Chicago today and goes by another name, but I'm gonna tell you just like I told that other fellow who wanted to know about Solomon, we all colored folks together and we better look out for..."

"Other fellow? Mrs. James what other fellow?"

"Last week another fellow, Lee something-another, came by asking 'bout Solomon, so I told the story, and I told him we can't go make trouble for one another—just like I'm gonna tell you."

"Don't worry Mrs. James, that story is safe with me—it's the other fellow you may have to worry about." I got up and thanked Mrs. James for her hospitality.

Lee was playing me. He was setting me up for what I couldn't imagine. As I drove back through Lobeco, I decided to stop back by Arthur Breland's house. He told me that Lee had been to his house several days before me. He told Lee the same story, he told me, about Sarah and her family. I drove home laughing like a crazy man.

'That guy's a fraud," I said to Josephine, after I had told her everything.

"Lee seems to be such a nice man," Josephine said.

"He's a fraud and a northern confidence man. I just can't figure out his angle, I know he wants to write this book, but why did he have to string me along?"

"When he calls again, I'll tell him you're not in."

"Yeah, do that. I don't want anything to do with that guy any more."

After calling a few times and Josephine telling him that I was out, Lee called me at the college. I didn't tell him what I knew, only that I had changed my mind about working with him on this project. I wished him the best and hung up. I didn't hear anymore from him or about him for little over a year, then one evening the phone rings. It was Aunt Cora; she was out of breath with excitement. She told me that she was watching the Travis Smiley show and that there was a second-sighted black man on the show named Lee Jordan who told the story of Sarah Breland among other strange tales. There was a white woman on the show with Lee, who was introduced as his investigator and collaborator. This woman witnessed his séance and recorded them. She confirmed everything that he revealed about his experiences, having the dead use him as a vessel to communicate some dissatisfaction from their past lives. Aunt Cora said that she remembered me asking about the Brelands and wondered if there was any connection. I told her that there was none. I reminded her that this was the fellow who owns the herbal shop she suggested. Aunt Cora didn't remember ever meeting Lee. She knew about the herbal shop in town, but she bought her ginger tea from the GNC store in the mall. Josephine may have seen the place and thought it closer than the mall, I surmised. "Anyway," Aunt Cora continued, "He's written a best selling book, called 'The Man Who Heard the Dead.'"

GHETTO STAR

It was never a surprise to me that things turned out as they did for Earl Lewis, but let me call him Blue, so everybody who reads the newspapers will know who I'm talking about. I could see it coming even before Blue was old enough to navigate the streets of North Charleston. I knew that boy was gonna be a cool slickster, a rich hustler, a tough gangster, and a troubled soul. I must admit that I had the advantage of knowing Blue's family history. I know his mama and his grandma. I knew his daddy and his grand daddy. And, I lived in New York City for a while where I learned to detect underworld characteristics and where I gained extensive knowledge about some enterprising hustlers. I witnessed the gangster star of Nicky Barnes burn out over the New York City sky. I say all of this to qualify my talent at identifying the upright from the crooked, the straight from the narrow, the slick from the unslick.

Besides my insightful scholarship on the gamester vocation, I, too, have a short personal history. I once thought of myself as a slickster, an illusion that cost me three years in the penitentiary. I missed the call on myself, but even before little Earl Lewis got into middle school, where they started calling him Blue, I could tell that he was gonna be a slick hustling racketeer; a gangster. Everything it takes to be slick was developing in that boy. He was charming, amiable, deviant, tough, resourceful, commanding, and he rejected being treated like the chumps Don Vito Corleone described to his son Michael in the movie, The Godfather. He was charismatic and he had the aura of success stamped on his persona. He grew up to be a handsome young man with clear tan skin and bright brown eyes. At the height of his career, Blue had obtained celebrity status in the streets of Charleston and beyond. He was not a movie star, nor a hip-hop rapper. He was not a sports figure, nor a politician, but Blue enchanted everyone he met. He was one of them—from the streets—he was a ghetto star.

Then there is the history of his family.

I grew up in the North Area where Blue's grandparents, Gladys and Harold Lewis were bootleggers. They sold liquor from their great big house over on Greenhaven Street. I started going by there with my friends when we were in our mid-teens to buy some hooch. Their house is across the railroad tracks. The first house beyond the gas station. It was then a well-kept two-story brick house with four bedrooms upstairs and six super large rooms on the ground floor. This was the first house I'd been in with more than one bathroom. It was the best looking and the most popular house in the neighborhood until the old man died. They sold store bought-liquor for a marked up price and corn liquor; people called scrap iron, which they bought from a man who lived way out in the country. And, there was always a card game or two going on. Now you gotta understand, these weren't bad people, just people trying to make a way for themselves in the racial atmosphere of the fifties' South. Most hustlers don't consciously intend society any grief, it just happens that way when it does. They did what they did and didn't see any criminality to it. In fact, Gladys and Harold Lewis were highly respected and admired. They were respected for the financial help they gave to many of their neighbors and admired for their business accomplishments.

For many years, Gladys and Harold didn't have any children. They were told that Gladys couldn't conceive. Then in early 1956, at the age of thirty-three, Gladys became pregnant. They had a girl they named Pearl. Business was good and now the Lewis' had someone to lavish their good fortune on. Young Pearl grew up a privileged child without any knowledge of what her parents did for a living. She was kept away from it. Pearl was nine years old when her father died of a massive heart attack on the same day that Malcolm X was assassinated. February 21, 1965 was a bone cold day in lots of ways. I remember the cold and the anguish because I was living in New York City back then.

Anyway, after her husband died, Gladys quit the bootleg business and the gambling. Gladys and Harold had family in Detroit, Chicago, Cleveland, Philadelphia, and New York City. All of them had friends from the Charleston area who needed boarding when they visited. They convinced Gladys that she should turn her home into a boarding house. They sent Gladys boarders year-round from all of those big northern cities. In the summer when many family reunions were held, Gladys had to turn boarders away. Gladys was a great cook and this probably added to the popularity of her boarding house.

During a week of civil rights protest in Charleston, in June of 1967, Jesse Jackson stayed at Gladys' boarding house. In death, Harold Lewis' memory took on legendary proportions in the neighborhood and throughout the North Area. People all over the county reminisced about the outrageous exploits and celebrated drinking bouts, real and imaginary, that took place at the "Big House." Even Gladys was flustered by the lies some people promoted. Because of Gladys' success in the boarding business, her celebrity became more renown. She was the neighborhood's example of the widow who turned adversity into victory. She was like the queen of the neighborhood and her cute little daughter Pearl was the princess. They went to church together every Sunday, and were, for the most part, inseparable icons of the neighborhood. So Pearl never knew but what she heard about her parents past activities.

Pearl grew up during the turmoil of the civil rights movement, but what remained with her most was the fight for integrated schools in South Carolina in general and Charleston in particular. Living in the insular black world of the North Area, she was mostly untouched by the harshest traditional bias, but she was forever scarred by the fierce tension in the newly integrated high school she attended. She summoned the courage to get through the experience with grades good enough to propel her on to college. Pearl finished her first year in college with a 3.5 grade average. She would have sailed through the next three years of college if she never met Barry Nelson, an attractive charming man, sixteen years her senior. They met literally by accident one morning while Pearl was driving to a class. Barry wasn't paying attention to his driving and bumped Pearl's car while she sat at a light. When they got out of their cars to assess their damages, Barry was stuck dead with Pearl's good looks. Her smooth caramel colored skin, long black hair, her youthful comely body and her pretty face. He apologized for hitting her car and they exchanged insurance information and addresses although there was no apparent damage to either car. Pearl was also kind of taken with Barry. He was good looking and had the air and speech of a successful out-of-towner. Plus, he was driving a 1974 Mercedes-Benz.

Barry Nelson was thirty-four years old when he first met Pearl Lewis. He was born in Charleston but was raised in New York City by his mother who fled the South with her two children when her husband became overbearing, non-supportive and violent. Barry, his sister and their mother moved to the South Bronx in 1950. Since they had a large family back in Charleston, Barry's mother got him out of the troubled streets of the South Bronx during school break by sending him to live with relatives in Charleston in the summers. Barry grew up knowing the streets of Charleston as well as he knew the streets of the South Bronx. In 1973, when Barry relocated to Charleston to start up his own numbers racket; he was already acquainted with the city and the people. He grew up working in the Bronx division of the numbers racket of Spanish Raymond, the numbers king from East Harlem. Barry learned all there was to learn about the numbers racket and he had saved his money to realize his dream of one-day being a numbers kingpin. At the time, there weren't any numbers game in Charleston. Barry understood the huge risks of introducing a mostly black participant racket to the South, but he also knew that the rewards would be immensely enriching.

When Barry and Pearl had their first accident, there were others to come; Barry was well on his way to establishing his numbers empire. He had three spots in the city and seven out in the country operating as numbers parlors. Each spot was averaging a grand a week; sixty percent of that went to Barry. The evening of the accident, Barry showed up at the big house across the railroad tracks. He introduced himself to Gladys and explained that his visit was to make sure that Pearl was unhurt after their accident. Gladys called Pearl to the parlor and left the two alone. They made small talk for a while, kind of sizing each other up. Then Barry asked Pearl out for dinner. In two days, Barry was in those drawers. In two months Pearl was in a BMW. In three months, Barry won over the admiration and confidence of Gladys, who saw a lot of her husband in Barry.

In four months Pearl turned nineteen. In five months, she was pregnant. This was their second accident. In fourteen months, Earl Lewis was born. In twenty-four months, the romance was over.

Marriage was not in the cards for them. The baby didn't even get his father's last name. Pearl didn't go back to college after the baby's birth, instead she completed a course at a cosmetology school and with Barry's financial help she opened up a beauty salon. In a few years, Barry opened another five numbers parlors and the money was flowing. His relationship with Pearl had soured mostly because Barry had women all over this city and in New York. Barry loved and cared for his son. He took Earl out every Saturday morning, and he provided anything Pearl wanted for the boy.

Word of Barry's success had spread to dark quarters in an envious way. Some resentful local slicksters and their allies in New York desired what Barry had built. They conspired silently and secretively. One evening walking alone from a popular restaurant to his car, a drive-by shooter gunned down Barry. This was Barry's final accident. The accuracy of my description of the incident as an accident is as questionable as the accident of life. This was in 1980 when Earl Lewis was five years old. I had just been released from a New York State penitentiary. I moved back to Charleston and started up my limousine service.

I joined the army in 1960 to get out of Charleston. I was eighteen years old. Most of my service was spent over seas in Germany. In 1963, I received an honorable discharge at an army demarcation station in New York City. I stayed there for a few weeks before I came back home to Charleston. After a while, I decided to go back to live in the land of opportunity. It was in New York that I first met Barry Nelson and it was there that the brief history with the underworld I alluded too began. Let me ease into it this way: I have a friend, who while drunk, years ago, fell on the tracks while waiting for a train in a Harlem subway station. The train blared into the station before my friend could fully recover and remove his entire body away from the tracks. The wheels of the train severed his left leg at the knee. Whenever curious children or adults with bad manners, inquired about my friend's missing limb, in a deep dark, mysterious voice, he always explained, that a dragon bit it off. I think my friend's dramatic metaphor is a pragmatic path to the truth that spares one the annoyance of details, so whenever I talk about the events that led up to my incarceration I prefer to use a similar contrivance. I tell the story of my short flirtation with the underworld by reciting a rhyme I learned in the joint.

Honky Tonk Bud
The hip cat stud
Stood digging a game of pool
He wasn't bragging, but his bags were bagging
And he was feeling pretty cool
He was choked up tight in a white on white
And a cocoa brown that was down
A green slim tie slung to his fly
And he sported a gold dust crown.
It was the fifth frame of a nine-ball game
When from the corner of his eye
Old Honky suddenly spied
A strange looking dude walking his way
He was a funny built cat
Wore a funny style hat
Looked to be 'bout three years old

And as the cat moved in
Old Honky kind of grinned
'Cause he shivered like he was cold
He wanted to know where Joe's at?
Honky said Joe's not ' round, 'cause his bags are down
And he went to his man to score
But if you got eyes for copping some coke
Like I can cop for you
I'm Honky Tonk Bud
The hip cat stud
From Lenox Avenue.
And in five minutes flat
Old Honky was back
They stood over in a corner
And poured some smack
From a cellophane sack
Honky went into a nod and said
Jim, I'm high
The fellow flashed a gold badge and said
That's too bad
'Cause I'm the FBI
Now Honky's high was gone
And his trial was on
The gamers came from miles 'round
To see how they were gonna put old Honky down
There was Cabbage Head Ned
Who got busted by the Feds
Fifty hoes from off the streets
Came dressed real neat
To say their final farewell.
The judge said Mr. Bud do you have any last words?
Bud said yeah

THE DEVIL BEATS HIS WIFE

What about all those drunken villains
Who run over your children
Pay a small fine and go free
Three years, the judge said
Slamming the wooden gravel down.

The rhyme is recited again telling the story of Bud's life on his release from jail. The scene replays itself; he's back at the same pool hall, watching another nine-ball game. He's dressed the same as he was before. The same strange looking dude approaches him. The whole thing happens to Bud again. Only this time when Bud is asked where Joe was, He says "Baby I don't even know who Joe is." And this, for me is the meaning of redemption and reform, I picked up on this lesson many slickers never learn. I brought my little stash of cash to Charleston, registered my limousine service under the name Buddy Chapman, and set out to earn an honest living. I got reacquainted with the town and the people in no time. I picked up on all that I had missed out on and started off from where I left off—just like I never was gone.

Earl had a small crew hustling reefers for him in middle school as early as 1990. His chief of operations was a popular white boy named Brad Middleton, but everybody called him Whiteboy. Earl and Brad became friends in the third grade and stayed tight ever since. Brad had lots of black friends who would always refer to him as the white boy; this stuck and became Whiteboy. This is how he was addressed, but it was assent racial overtones. Earl had a Michael Jordan tee shirt printed on a blue background that he wore so often people wondered if it was ever washed. They didn't know that Earl had several of them. Anyway, kids looking to buy some reefers would inquire about the boy with the blue Michael Jordan tee shirt or the boy in the blue tee shirt. In their desire to be cryptic, reefer seekers started asking "You seen Blue?" Earl Lewis received his street name and a reputation in middle school that would mark him for all his future.

While in his second year of high school, Blue learned the value of insulating himself from his operation. His favorite movies were The Godfather and New Jack City. Blue viewed himself as a fusion of Nino Brown and Michael Corleone, two fictional gangsters who represented the reality he wanted to live. His goal was to develop a few trusted lieutenants who would direct his crew leaders. The crew leaders would manage his legion of foot soldiers. Whiteboy would be the link between Blue and his lieutenants. Whiteboy recruited David Wesley, another white boy who was selling a little pot West of the Ashley. David was a big boy for sixteen; he was extremely strong and had a violent temper. David Wesley was known as Fish and was thought capable of anything. Fish got his supply of marijuana from Blue free for handling problems here and there. He would be the organization's internal and external enforcer. Blue selected three African American boys, all from different areas of the city, for the top echelon of his organization.

Hold on for a minute.

While I was in the joint, I grew to dislike the term "African American." I don't like to use it and I don't like to hear it used. This isn't because I feel it's an inappropriate way to describe black Americans, no that's not the case at all. I don't care for it because it's a mouth full to say—African American. You would think that I should be contented with the designation given all the others things we've been called in the last three hundred years, but I feel it's time to cut through the chase. In America, when we talk about an Italian American, or a Jewish

American, or an Irish American, or an American from Puerto Rico, we say the Italian guy, or the Jewish guy, or the Irish guy, or the Puerto Rican. With all these groups the "American" is a given. What about the African guy? Can the American ever be a given for the African guy?

Anyway, the three African kids were all tough boys from the streets; either Blue or Whiteboy had known one or the other of them for some years. Julia Payne, a large white girl with braided hair, a foul mouth, an inner-city attitude and who was also widely known as Mama Love, joined Billy Brown, Antawarn Whither, and Ernest Jones as the four corners of Blue's empire. Each captain would recruit crew leaders who would enlist street dealers from their neighborhood, but they all had to receive Whiteboy's approval. Billy Brown was called Dollar Bill. The neighborhood on the eastside of Ashley Phosphate Road, near the mall, was his turf. Billy was seventeen and in the eleventh grade. He had two crew leaders and six dealers. Antawarn Whither was eighteen and a senior in high school. He had three crew leaders and ten dealers West of the Ashley. Since his turf was away from the North Area, Antawarn had more autonomy running his operation. This would later be the source of many conflicts and a fatal confrontation. Ernest Jones, known as Jo-Jo, operated in the Liberty Park area with four crew leaders and twelve street dealers. Jo-Jo was sixteen and in the eleventh grade. Mama Love had two crew leaders with four dealers in the Naval Base area and three crew leaders with ten dealers in the Cosgrove neighborhood. Mama Love was nineteen years old and graduated from high school the year before. The whole syndicate was known as the Blue Crew and it was the third largest marijuana dealing operation in the Charleston Metropolitan area, nearly entirely comprised of high school students.

When this all became reality, Blue was still living at home with Pearl and Gladys. He was seventeen and in the eleventh grade. They knew from the volume of activity that Blue was into some kind of hustle, but he was attending school and getting the kinds of grades that made him college bound. Blue was one of the most popular kids in school and in the neighborhoods of the city. The people Pearl and Gladys saw around Blue, all created an air of suspicion, but they were all high school kids, who by nature, are suppose to be mysterious. Beside, Blue had never been in any trouble with the law. He would get a traffic ticket now and then, but that had been it. Pearl was busy with her salon which had grown popular and had expanded into the hair braiding and extension business. She was nearing forty and seeing a married city councilman. Gladys was in her seventies. She didn't get many boarders these days. She spent most of her time cleaning, cooking, and watching television. So Blue was pretty much in his own custody, his family tutelage was on autopilot, so long as there were no problems.

Blue loved music and basketball. He studied music theory in middle and high school and he played the drums, but he never had the time or the desire to pursue a career in music. Blue met a popular ex-radio disc jockey, who called himself the Screaming Eagle. He was a man who flirted on the fringe of the drug culture, but he was also establishing his own small record label and had been successful as a concert promoter. A mutual friend at a local club introduced Blue to the Eagle. They talked about the entertainment business in general and the money that could be generated producing records and promoting concerts. Blue was impressed by the Eagle's knowledge and by the big names he had brought to Charleston for concerts. The Eagle hoped to lure some of those big names to his label, but he was also interested in developing new talents. He was already developing acts from South Carolina, Georgia, and North Carolina. The Eagle knew all the rumors about Blue and his reefer empire. He didn't say it outright, but he insinuated that an investment in his enterprises would be a way to clean up some of Blue's money. Then he invited Blue to his home for a more formal meeting.

The meeting took place a week later. The Eagle's home was large and well decorated. He had four young ladies at his house when Blue arrived. The girls were all well dressed and lovely, and while they were all older than Blue, they flirted with him and he flirted back. The disc player dispensed light jazz and hip-hop music that set a pleasant mood. There was food from a well-respected Caribbean restaurant on a foldout table. They talked, flirted, and ate. The Eagle pulled out some coke, which they snorted and Blue gave up a few joints and they smoked. When it was time for them to talk, the Eagle and Blue excused themselves from the young ladies. Blue was led back to the study. The room was laden with books and pictures of the Eagle with the many stars he had promoted in the Charleston area. Blue was dazzled. The Nino Brown in him saw style and opportunity. The Michael Corleone in him saw acquisition and expansion. Blue agreed to a deal to help finance the Eagles enterprises. Blue was, in the beginning, a silent partner, but he did get charge of some minor assignments.

Blue took charge of making the transportation arrangements for the performers while they were in town. This gave Blue a chance to meet the performers, some of whom asked straight away for reefer or cocaine. Blue provided the reefer but had to make other arrangements to get the more expensive drug for his celebrity clients. It was during this period that we became better acquainted. Whenever he came by to make travel arrangements, I'd hold his attention with stories about the old days. I recalled stories about his dad and his grand dad and the legends they became to street people. I'd make him laugh about my time as a small time cocaine dealer and my time in a New York penitentiary. Blue took a liking to me and would often come by just to talk. I received a lot of business through their concerts, so it was in my best interests that our relationship be personal. Besides, I liked the boy; he had charmed me too. Blue confided in me like a trusted counselor. He told me all about the meeting he held with his gang after the Miami trip.

Blue graduated from high school in June of 1992. That weekend he and Whiteboy drove to Miami to meet with a Colombian man. Blue's marijuana supplier had introduced Whiteboy to the man in a Charleston bar the month before the trip. The Colombian had cocaine connections. He had been in Charleston on a delivery mission and to find people to expand his operations in the area. Blue and Whiteboy drove to Miami unarmed and unafraid. They stayed at a four-star hotel and were wined and dined by their host. The negotiations went smoothly and to their satisfaction. They would receive cash on delivery shipments of cocaine in Charleston. A line of communications was set up and a shipment price was established. They drove home stimulated by the danger of the trip and excited by the new plans.

The weekend after the Miami trip, Blue met with Whiteboy and his captains in Myrtle Beach to celebrate graduation and to explain the changes he had planned for the organization. The meeting was scheduled for the first of the two nights at Myrtle Beach. Everyone, except Blue, was at Whiteboy's hotel room early for the meeting. They all grilled Whiteboy about the mystery, but he resisted telling them anything by saying they should wait for their leader. Finally, there was a knock on the door. It was Blue in a particularly dramatic mood. Tonight he was Nino Brown, stylish and spectacular. He was dressed in a black two-piece collarless silk suit, over a beige crewneck sweater. He wore black sandals without socks. Blue greeted everyone with hugs and playful pats. He kissed Mama Love on the lips and she playfully grabbed his ass.

"Did my man say anything to y'all about the purpose of this meeting," Blue asked referring to Whiteboy.

Everybody nodded or said no.

"No Whiteboy tighter than a clam," Antawarn said.

"Well everybody sit down," Blue said. "You got anything here to eat and drink?" He asked Whiteboy.

"Pizza and Killians."

"Well alright, break it out and let's get started."

Whiteboy handed everyone a beer from the refrigerator. He went to the small kitchen area, picked up the top box of pizza and put it on the coffee table. Blue took a sip from his beer and put the bottle on a lamp table.

"Here is the deal." He took a tiny empty cellophane envelope with a blue dot on it from his pocket. Blue handed the envelope to Mama Love.

"Pass it around."

"Man what we gonna do with this?" Antawarn asked, as the envelope reached him. "This shit's too small to even put enough reefer in it for a joint."

"Our reefer days are over Dog. We are gonna switch our street dealers from smoke to coke," Blue said. "You know what that blue dot means?"

"That's our brand," Mama Love said.

"That's my brand and I don't want any of you to ever forget that shit," Blue snarled. Then he handed everyone an envelope like the one that was passed around, only these envelopes had a powder in them.

There was a long silence. No one said anything. Then Mama Love used her fingernails to open her envelope. She took the same fingernail to scoop up some of the powder to her nostril, then some to the other nostril. She made a loud snorting sound pulling the powder into her nose, her eyes went around, and she swallowed and made a face like her saliva was bitter. All the others followed her lead and for a few minutes, there was only the sound of snorting.

"Good shit", Blue said, "and we got the connect. I've got weight for all of you after we get back from our weekend party."

"Now we really got to watch our backs," Antawarn said. "There's a lot more time that goes with this crime."

"Just stay cool," Whiteboy said. "The part of this change we need to worry about is the other crews out there doing their thing. We can operate around the police, but we don't want to create any conflicts with other people out there making a living."

"We don't want any trouble," Blue said, "but we won't back down. We've got a right to make a living too." After Blue dispensed some more details and kind of a corporate motivational pep talk, the meeting ended and they all went out to enjoy the nightlife at Myrtle Beach.

The new merchandise went into the supply line on their return to Charleston. The transition went smoothly, but everyone was surprised by the huge increase in cash the cocaine brought. Everybody's percent of the take stayed the same as it was before, but the money they received tripled, and they found ways to spend it. The Eagle helped Blue to get a two-bedroom condominium in Mount Pleasant. Shortly after that, Blue bought a brand new blue and white BMW. All his people were doing well and the Charleston economy could feel it. On Saturday evenings, the street dealers left their hangs to get clean for the night. They would, nearly all of them, be in Regal's department store shopping for the most expensive name-brand outfits. They shopped for the latest inner-city fad clothing and they didn't care about the cost. It was easy to tell who they were; they were always loud, uncouth and they displayed erratic street demeanor. They had an awkwardness that brought them attention as they hovered over a table of goods like buzzards over a piece of road kill. When they went to the cashiers, they'd pull out wads of cash so huge the cashier's mouth watered. Their cellular telephones rang all the time and they rudely told callers that they would be right there. Still, the sales clerks at Regal's were happy to serve them because the sales were mostly quick and provided a good commission.

I was in Regal's one evening doing some shopping and watching the drug dealers grab and buy. I was over in the suit department looking at suits. The shoe department is across from the suits. I was near the aisle where people move from one department to another. I noticed an attractive young African couple walking at a brisk pace to the next department. Behind them was a bright skinned, little African girl, maybe five years old. The couple walked so fast that they left the child far behind. Young people are so inattentive I thought I'd better help out. I called out to the couple that they were leaving their child behind. They turned around, gave me a blank stare and kept on walking. A young white woman, who was in the shoe department near where the child stood, looked me in the eyes as she caressed the child's hand and loudly declared the child her own. I stood embarrassed, but how was I to know? When it comes to race, I'm from a not so distant dimension in the past. On the question of race, there had been no significant movement in a hundred years, and then there was a great leap in a relatively short space of time. In today's world, one never knows.

Blue had as many white girl friends as African ones. He took them to public places without incident. He even knew some of their parents and was welcomed into their homes. Something as normal as the mornings light to this post civil rights new breed. I'm continually astonished by it all. I see these young white people in the malls who look, dress, and talk like African kids, even down to the cornrows. I look at television and I see Africans in high place in business, medicine, and government; there is even an African man who is the director of the Museum of Natural History in New York City. Then I see the Republican Party replacing the Confederate flag as the magnet for racist white voter's need for racial exclusivity. And, I read where seventy percent of Africans in colleges are female. Violence, drugs and jails are destroying too many young African males. The whole thing is enigmatic and disorienting for a man of my generation.

Greed is a mischievous thing. Blue always treated Antawarn fairly. Whenever Antawarn needed an extra package, over the three or four years that they had moved over to cocaine, Blue got it to him. All the many times Antawarn's account came up a little short and Whiteboy wanted to cut him loose, Blue stepped in, noted the event and then let it pass, forgotten. So, it was a surprise to Blue when Whiteboy told him that Antawarn wanted out of the organization to run his own operation West of the Ashley. Blue got Whiteboy to set up a meeting with Antawarn, but he wanted to handle this situation personally. Antawarn had always been the most out spoken of his captains and he often acted as if he spoke for them all. Blue wanted to assess Antawarn's influence on the other captains and eliminate it. Blue loved the many intrigues of gangsterism; he had Whiteboy to set the meeting for early morning. Blue met with Antawarn early on a Monday morning, at a pool-hall in Antawarn's neighborhood. Antawarn wanted to discuss business right on the floor with ten other people, some of them outsiders, playing pool and lounging around, but Blue was able to convince him to take a ride to talk. The conversation took place as Blue drove slowly around Citadel Mall. Antawarn was disrespectful, hostile and bent on bolting from Blue's crew. He was blunt about not wanting to turn over money to anybody when he could be his own man. He told Blue that he had other contacts and that West Ashley was his territory. This was Antawarn's position and he was adamant about it. Blue spoke like an arbitrator. He reminded Antawarn of how he had nothing when he got involved with the crew. He recalled many of the ways he had helped Antawarn's troubled family. He told Antawarn about all the money that he knew Antawarn had withheld. Blue said that he only wanted Antawarn's loyalty. Then Blue asked Antawarn not to make a move until he had time to consider another arrangement what would increase Antawarn's take. Antawarn only agreed after Blue assured him that it would only take a couple of days. Blue insisted they have lunch together. Blue guided the lunch conversation to sports, music and girls. Half way through lunch, the earlier tension had disappeared and the two antagonists laughed together. After lunch, Blue drove Antawarn back to the pool hall. Don Corleone was smooth and deceptive.

During the rest of the day, Blue met individually with the other captains. He drove to where he knew each would be hanging out and engaged in idle conversation. Blue wanted to see if anyone would volunteer anything on Antawarn and he wanted to sniff out any dissension. After he met with everyone, Blue drove toward his grandma's house. Blue called Fish from his cellular telephone. He told Fish to meet him at Wet Willie's, a bar in Blue's old neighborhood. Then he called Mike Douglas, one of Antawarn's crew leaders, and asked him to meet him at the bar. Blue knew Mike, who was older than most of the people in the organization, to be resentful and ambitious. These were emotions he could use against Antawarn. Blue asked Mike to be prompt and discreet.

Blue sat in a red plastic-covered booth in the corner near the kitchen door. Two guys played at the pool table. There was a couple drinking at the bar and a group of workers eating at a table near the door. Fish came into the bar, looked around until he spotted Blue. Fish is a two hundred and twenty-pound, tomato-face weight lifter. He was dressed in an oversized denim Fubu outfit and an X cap left over from the Spike Lee movie. Fish is a lot more jovial than others portray him. He approached Blue with a big Irish smile on his face. Blue didn't return the smile. He gestured for Fish to sit down. "I got something for you," Blue said getting right to the point.

"That's why I'm here," Fish said. "Whip it on me."

"Antawarn is out of line."

"Where you want him?"

"Hospitalized."

"When?"

"Yesterday"

"Got ya'—Later."

"I want him to know who sent you."

Fish got up to leave and passed by Mike Douglas who had just entered the bar and was headed towards the booth. Mike looked like he was forming a question about the beefy white boy that was just leaving Blue's booth, but he thought it better just to note it in his mind and not get inquisitive. "Hey Blue, you look good man," Mike said.

"You look good too, Dog—sit down."

"Thank you brother."

"You want something to eat or drink?"

"A hamburger, some fries and a root beer soda."

Blue called the waitress over and ordered hamburgers, fries and sodas for himself and for Mike.

"What is your favorite movie?" Blue asked.

"I don't have a favorite movie, but I dig Samuel L. Jackson and the flicks he be in."

"Oh yeah, which are his best movies?"

"Man, I don't know. I like when he plays a gangster. Sam Jackson plays a mean gangster—his shit is real. He was bad in Pulp Fiction and in Jackie Brown—he busted that bad gangster role in both of those flicks."

"Did you see him play the junkie in Jungle Fever?"

"Yeah, I didn't know who he was then, but I could tell that he was real. There's something about that dude that's straight out of the streets."

"Look Mike, the next time Whiteboy brings a package to this area, he's going to give it to you. Can you get the people together to handle it?

"What about Antawarn?"

"Antawarn is out—don't you worry about him. You concentrate on moving the package. Now, can you move it?"

"What my cut?"

"The same as Antawarn. Can you move it?"

"Here comes the burgers. Hey Blue I feel like I just got a raise. I can move your package. Let me pay for the lunch huh?"

"Whiteboy will work things out with you about pick ups

and drops. If I knew you were going to pay I would have had a steak."

Fish knew where Antawarn lived and he knew about the pool hall where he hung out, but he didn't know what time he went home. Fish had a handful of stringers he could depend on. He called a boy known as The Black Bishop. He put The Black Bishop on Antawarn to find out the best time to surprise him. Two evenings later, Fish picked up The Black Bishop and a twenty-year-old white boy named Carl Sanchez. Fish drives a red pick up truck with a Confederate flag plate in the front. The Confederate flag means different things to different people. Fish perceives it as making a tough-guy anti-social statement. He overlooks the racial aspect of the flag's symbol. He likes that fact that in the movies the guys with the Confederate flag are always beating up young Forrest Gump, or somebody. The Black Bishop reported that Antawarn goes to Pringles Home Cooking restaurant for dinner about eight o'clock. While Fish drove to the restaurant, he explained what the job was; they just wanted to break a few ribs and mess up Antawarn's face. Pringles is on Spring Street and it's a detached building that sits back from the street. It has a dirt parking lot in front and is surrounded by old trees. The parking lot has two-security lights, but the heavy top foliage on the trees blocked the light from going through and left the lower part of the lot dark and shadowy. Fish parked his truck at the entrance to the lot, where he had a view of the entire lot. He positioned his two armed stringers on each side of the darkened parking lot.

Antawarn arrived shortly after Fish and his crew got into position. When he got out of his car, the two stringers quickly approached him with their guns drawn. They grabbed the startled dope dealer's arms and led him towards the red pick up truck. Fish started the truck up, but left the lights off.

When the stringers got Antawarn to the truck, Fish handed them real handcuffs and they placed them on Antawarn, before they helped him into the truck. Fish drove out of the parking lot before he put the lights of the truck on. The Black Bishop rode in the back of the truck. Antawarn set between the two white boys with a gun pointed to his chest. "What's this about?" he asked.

"You'll find out when we get there." Fish said, as he drove into traffic. "Now I don't wanna hear no mo' shit from ya'."

"Look what ya'll want—money?"

"I said shut the fuck up,' Fish hollered, and Carl lifted the gun up to Antawarn's mouth.

Antawarn didn't say anything else until they arrived out in the country and pulled down a dark secluded road. "So this is the way Blue wants it huh?" He said, resigned to his fate.

"This is the way Blue is gonna get it," Fish answered.

Fish turned the truck onto a dark road and drove for half a mile. He stopped the truck and turned the light off. Carl opened his door, as the Black Bishop jumped over the side of the truck. Fish got out and walked around to where the stringers held Antawarn. "Nothing personal brother," he said, as he sent a crushing blow to Antawarn's face. Fish hit Artiwarn twice in his rib section and the blows sent him reeling back against the truck, his weight taking the two that held him along. Fish stuck another blow to the face and Antawarn fell to the ground. They all kicked Antawarn several times in the ribs. Antawarn blacked out. Fish removed the handcuffs, ordered his helpers into the truck and they drove off leaving Antawarn curled up on the ground.

The phone rang. Blue picked up the receiver.

"Yeah."

"Hey Blue. Shit's all over the news. They found Antawarn

in the woods outside of town all bloodied and beaten up." Whiteboy said excitedly into the phone.

"No shit—must have ran up against a bear out there. That dude need to stay out the woods."

Whiteboy let out a chuckle.

"Meet me for breakfast in an hour. You know where."

Whiteboy met Blue at the Bagel Hut in Mount Pleasant. There is a section in the newspaper that covers the local crime beat. Every morning there is five or six short articles about the previous day's robberies, murders and swindles of an ordinary nature. I read it every day. This kind of mayhem makes me feel like I'm still in New York, the way these young thugs are killing each other. Spectacular versions of these same crimes get a more prominent space. Blue was reading the short article in the newspaper about the beating. The article ended stating that the police suspected that the beating was drug related although the victim said he couldn't identify his attackers. Whiteboy made clear, right off, that he disagreed with the way this problem was handled. "If you gonna start something, go all the way," were his actual words. He warned Blue that Antawarn wouldn't go away quietly and that some of his dealers would remain loyal to him. Blue had broken their credo and Whiteboy predicted it would come back to bite him. During breakfast Blue instructed Whiteboy to talk with all the street dealers under Antawarn to let them know that Mike Douglas was now in control of the West Ashley operation. Blue slid a package to Whiteboy and instructed him to give it to Mike Douglas.

Antawarn was released from the hospital in a few days. For the first two weeks after his release, there was a lot of tension in the streets, almost as if everyone was anticipating a big event. The word was out on the grapevine that Antawarn was looking for revenge. I saw Blue a few times during this period when street people were looking for the big showdown. Fish was driving him everywhere these days. The last time I saw him was when he came in to make arrangements for transportation for some big names they had coming to the city for a concert. I didn't sense any anxiety in his manner; he was his usual cool self. He was ecstatic about the concert at the Coliseum. The concert featured two of the biggest current names in hip-hop and a big name soul singer from the recent past. The show was heavily promoted on radio and on television for two weeks prior to the opening night. It was the most ambitious promotion they had done and it was sold out. Blue seemed proud to be a part of such a grand public event. We didn't discuss his problem, but I believe that he knew that I was aware of what was going on. After we finalized all the travel arrangements for the weekend, Blue gave me two tickets. I, at first, declined them, saying rap wasn't my thing, but Blue insisted and admonished me for resisting his generosity. Then he eased the tension by smilingly telling me that there would be some people there my age.

The concert was a loud rampage of sound, images, smoke and lights. I remember going to shows where the master of ceremony would introduce an act—the act would walk on the stage, the spotlight would come on and the act would do their thing—bang. This concert was nothing like that. The performers made spectacular entrances coming down from the ceiling accompanied by smoke and lights and thunderous noise. People swung from rope ladders and popped out of things. The performers romped around the entire stage hollering out their rhymes and getting the fans to join in a call and answer routine. The young audience danced, sang along and loved every minute of the show. During the intermission, the concession stands in the lobby were crowded with people eager to be seen in their new outfits bought especially for this occasion. When the show ended, no one seemed to want to leave. They milled around calling out to friends the names of clubs where they would meet and trying desperately to garner attention to themselves and their group.

The parking lot was filled with people talking, laughing and making plans for the rest of the evening. Blue returned from a quick meeting with the Screaming Eagle and some other associates to catch up to his entourage at the main entrance to the Coliseum. His limousine was waiting in a no parking zone. Whenever Blue rented a limousine from me, he always got the same white stretch deluxe and the same driver. He had an entourage of ten people including Fish and the Black Bishop who acted as security for Blue and his group. Blue gave them the signal to load up. He was taking them to an exclusive party at the hotel where the concert stars were staying. The main group stood by the car. Fish and the Black Bishop stood off from the car as the driver walked to the rear to open the doors. They heard the squeal of car tires, but before they could all turn towards the sound, gunshots rang out. It seemed to them that time froze into that single frame, but it was only seconds before the car drove between them and the two bodyguards spraying automatic gunfire from the rear seats. They all fell to the ground screaming as the darkened car sped off.

Fish had been hit in the shoulder. He struggled to get up as he called out to Blue. The Black Bishop was sprawled out dead. The others lay in a pile. Blood was everywhere. Two of the young ladies lay dead and the other two were screaming hysterically. The only man in the main group that got hit was Blue. He had a nasty looking bullet wound to his chest and another in his upper right thigh. He was in agony and unable to speak. Everyone was in a daze. As people from the parking lot ran to the scene, two of the men with the group slipped off, the other man walked back and forth holding his head and cussing. My driver telephoned 911. Fish lumbered over to the limousine, took a pillow from a seat and placed it under Blue's head. Blue's eyes were blank and his body shook. Fish took the gun from the Black Bishop's belt and his own and put them in a trashcan. In a short time, policemen, EMS vans, fire trucks and detectives littered the area.

This was not a story for the local crime section of the newspaper. This was front-page stuff with banner headlines for a week as the investigation unfolded. "Concert Promoter Gunned Down," is how the week started. Then, "Concert Promoter Drug Kingpin," by mid-week. By the end of the week it was: "The Blue Crew Controls Drug Gangs in Charleston." Sunday's paper carried a featured article on Blue, digging all the way back to the days of Gladys and Harold Lewis. The article divulged how Blue's father, Barry Nelson, introduced the numbers racket in Charleston. The article even mentioned Blue's mama's relationship with the married city councilman. It was a damming article that put the worst face on Blue's case and his family's history. This was a story that captured the public's interest and the news media did all it could to perpetuate the story. The local television news stations produced exposé's on the different personalities entangled in the incident. S.L.E.D. and the FBI did a far-reaching investigation of the entire matter. People talked and much of what they said was leaked out to the press, true or not.

Blue was charged, arrested and read his rights in his hospital bed, but he was too sick to be moved. A 24-hour guard was placed in his room. To keep the story hot, the news media speculated day after day about the date of Blue's trial.

Antawarn was arrested in Newark, New Jersey, and the search went on for his two accomplices. Fish was released from the hospital, arrested and jailed. Whiteboy and the top echelon of the Blue Crew were all taken into custody. Many of the street dealers were rounded up and jailed. The whole structure of the Blue Crew caved in and the newspapers exposed every detail. People in the general population were surprised that all this could have been going on right under their noses. People from the streets were surprised by how quickly and completely the whole organization was crushed.

I often wonder if I could have made a difference had I warned Blue of what was lurking up ahead for him. In some of our conversations, I praised his grand father and his father in a manner that he might have mistakenly interpreted for adulation. I listened to his exploits far too approvingly. It all kept my business close to his purse strings and made me feel in the loop, when I knew he was headed towards tragedy. Disaster, I could have said, is the only sure thing in the life of a gangster.

NATASHA

Natasha White was half asleep and half awake as she looked at her image in the window, her face against the glass, as the Greyhound bus cruised down the final darkened stretch of highway before it would enter Charleston. Her image thrown onto the glass from the overhead light disappeared in the light of passing traffic and reappeared in the darkness. The eighteen-year-old girl searched the round image of her plain, pimpled face and found a stranger on a mysterious journey. She had her mother's thin nose, but her father's full lips. Her brown hair appeared black in the window's reflection and her brown eyes looked shades darker. For a moment, Natasha fancied herself a light-skinned black woman. The thought fully awakens her. She turned from the window and sat up in her seat. Natasha straightened the flowery dime-store dress her mother bought her and began to worry about her appearance. There were fifteen other passengers on the bus, but Natasha was the only one awake this Saturday morning in 1979, too excited to eat or sleep.

Natasha was nearing the end of a grueling fourteen-hour bus trip from Moscow, West Virginia to Charleston, South Carolina. She was traveling to Charleston to spend the summer with her boyfriend Nicholas Hilgrown. Nicholas had gone to Charleston a year earlier to find work. He moved on the advice of his best buddy, Billy Joe Tucker, who had himself, gone on the suggestion of another hometown friend. The town of

Moscow was experiencing a renewed exodus of yet another generation of its young people. Natasha would be but the latest in the long list of young people migrating out of Moscow, a decaying town that had its day in the sun a hundred years earlier.

Nicholas had been in Charleston for three months before he wrote the first letter to Natasha. Her reply was so passionate and positive, Nicholas began to write to her every day. In the evenings when he returned to his room from work as an electrical apprentice, Nicholas drank a six-pack of beer as he wrote his letters. In each letter, he sent a dollar for her to save, so that in June when she graduated from high school, she could buy a bus ticket to join him in Charleston. Nicholas and Natasha first met at a youth hangout outside of Moscow, where the town's young people congregated to drink whiskey and use drugs. He was twenty-one and already a man, and she was a girl of fourteen. They became involved shortly thereafter despite the seven-year difference. Nicholas had a beat-up truck and kept pocket change to buy beer and street pills. In a town as barren as mid-seventies Moscow, Nicholas was an impressive figure in the minds of many young girls and the envy of many young boys. Natasha was astonished that he chose her; a plain faced, plump girl with skinny legs. He taught her to drive in his truck and a borrowed car. This all raised her status among her peers. She would be forever grateful to Nicholas, so she made an early decision to be committed to him forever. Now this resolution was paying off again—he was getting her out of Moscow.

Time seemed to pass slower and more anxiety built up in Natasha the closer the bus got to Charleston. Natasha leaned her face back on the window and became hypnotized by her image. She had memorized every word of all of the letters

Nicholas sent her. In her mind, Natasha recited the first letter from Nicholas asking her to come to join him. In the letter, he told her how much he missed her; that he had a job and was on his way to becoming an electrician. The letter said that he had a large apartment. He wanted to buy her things and take real good care of her. He told her that there were things to do and see in Charleston. He underlined the part that said that he had not looked at another girl all the months he had been gone and he asked her to remain true to him. He reminded her of their passion each time that they made love. He closed saying he loved her. Her heart thumped and she closed her eyes.

Alexandra White, Natasha's mother, agreed to her going to Charleston on the condition that she would return in August in time to begin the two-year course she had enrolled in at Moscow Community College. Alexandra had resisted the idea at first, out of a sense of parental duty. In truth, however, Alexandra knew that her daughter would not return even when Natasha had not known it yet herself. Alexandra's assertion that she wanted Natasha to attend college when she returned from Charleston, was a fabrication that shielded her from any feelings of maternal guilt. The situation was dire for her family in Moscow and there was absolutely no hope. Natasha's absence would ease things slightly by leaving a little more money to feed and clothe the other two children, who were sixteen and fifteen and still in school. Alexandra wanted to keep her family together, but her life had been hard in Moscow, where survival was the primary instinct. This was a development that would lighten her load.

Boris White, a backward, lazy drunkard, abandoned his family when Natasha, the oldest of their three children, was four years old. For generations, the men of Moscow supported their families by working jobs out of state. Boris left one day to find work in Maryland, so he could send money back home. They never heard from him again. Over the years, they would hear rumors from men who had returned home from work away in other states that Boris had been seen in Kentucky, or Virginia, or Ohio, or Maryland. Alexandra raised her son, Vladimir, and her two daughters, Anna and Natasha alone. Her only source of money was a small check from the state's home relief fund. The family lived in a small shack of a house in the worst section of an impoverished town of a poor western county, of the poor state of West Virginia. Alexandra hoped that Natasha would not return to this, for her own sake and for the sake of her family.

Moscow, West Virginia was once a nameless coal mining area before the break from Virginia. The eastern areas of Virginia had the free labor of tens of thousands of slaves that made it productive and gave it supremacy over the western counties of the state. Moscow County was formed after the turmoil that highlighted the inequities that caused the western portion of Virginia to form its own state government. In 1863, President Lincoln and the United States Congress gave recognition to the newly created state of West Virginia. Shortly thereafter, a delegation of coal mining experts from Moscow, Russia came to the region to share in the development of a new coal removal technique with an American enterprise named Borman Coal Company. Count Dimitri Gorki, an influential bureaucrat in the Russian government, led the delegation of Russian mining experts and their wives. This alliance went on for more than twenty years and ended in a failed experiment. In the first year, a large community built up around the mining area, as men came for jobs in the mines and their families followed. The leaders at Borman Mining Company used their influence with the new State Legislature to flatter the Russians by getting the county named Moscow. The area that had built up around the mines grew into the town of Moscow.

All of the members of the Russian delegation were a curiosity to the people drawn to the area by the opportunity to work. They were impressed by the oddity of these strange people with mysterious sounding names from far away. Count Dimitri Gorki, an extremely refined gentleman and a member of the Russian aristocracy, made the biggest impression on the people. He was a great sensation everywhere that he appeared. A young man, who worked in the mines and once saw the Count in person, was so impressed by the man that he named his first son Dimiti. This started the trend of Russian named American children in Moscow, West Virginia, a newly formed American town named after a Russian city, so ancient, no one knows the date of its origin. Not every family followed the practice, but just the same, fifty or so Russian names reappeared generation after generation. By the time of the second Great War, knowledge of the history of the practice had grown dormant for most of the people of Moscow. Now, the Russian names reappears merely because people want to name their children after an ancestor.

It was near daybreak when the bus entered the outer stretches of Charleston. The streetlights were still on and offered a strange contrast with the early light of dawn. The boulevard was adorned with big neat houses and cars filled the tree-lined streets. Even these half-century-old homes looked new and captivating to Natasha. She thought she would burst with the excitement of seeing this New World and the knowledge that Nicholas was at the bus station not very far away waiting for her. Natasha took out her comb and looked in the window, but the dawn had stolen her reflection. She got up from her seat and walked to the restroom to freshen up. Natasha returned to her seat with an invigorated, but temporary sense of confidence. Her eyes eagerly drank in the sights. The bus driver's voice came over the intercom announcing its arrival into the city of Charleston, South Carolina. They were minutes away from the bus station. Natasha went numb. She was overwhelmed by emotions. She shook and shimmied in her seat. The whole experience became surreal to her, as if she were watching a scene from a movie. The bus pulled into the station and moved slowly toward the parking dock.

The bus came to a stop and the doors opened with a release of air. People rose to get their belongings and began filing off the bus. The driver was already down by the luggage hole with the door opened. Natasha was still seated. She looked through the window and saw the crowd around the luggage compartment. People who came to meet them at the station were greeting some of her fellow passengers. They hugged and kissed as they walked into the waiting room and towards the door that led to the street. She grabbed up the bag she brought with some sandwiches and now hot cans of sodas. During the entire trip she ate one sandwich and she drank one can of soda. Natasha finally got to the aisle and began to walk forward to the door, all the time looking out the windows searching for that familiar face. By the time she reached the luggage compartment, all the other passengers were gone from the loading deck.

"Is everything alright?" The driver asked as he handed the last suitcase from the luggage compartment to Natasha. "You look really frightened"

Natasha said nothing. She grabbed the soft black case by the pulling handle and looked nervously at the ground. She was terrified at the prospect that Nicholas might not come to pick her up and that this whole thing might be a cruel hoax.

"Somebody was supposed to meet you here?" The driver asked with a concerned look on his face. "You know it's early in the morning. It's six-thirty-two," he said looking at his pocket watch. "This is the start of the morning rush hour in Charleston and they could be stuck in traffic. Why don't you go into the waiting room, I'm sure they will be along shortly. Besides there's a telephone in there, maybe you could call someone."

The driver took Natasha by one elbow and led her to the waiting room door. He let her elbow loose to open the door. Two men were sprawled out on the benches to the side of the ticket window. The bus driver looked at them in dismay, but Natasha recognized one of them even in that slouching position. "Thank you," she said to the driver and walked over to the two men stretched out on the benches. The driver watched her for a moment, and then he disappeared into the dispatcher's office. As she approached, she could smell the stench of stale whiskey and beer stagnate in the air around the two men. Natasha touched the shoulder of one of the men saying softly "Nicky, Nicky." The figure came awake. Slowly he opened his eyes, and then he jumped up with loud excitement, grabbed Natasha up, and twirled her around. The commotion awoke his companion. "Wha' the fuck's going on?" He asked bewildered and unsteady. Nicholas and Natasha were kissing and making merriment in between cries of "Baby, baby, you're here, you're here." Nicholas put Natasha down and held her at arm's length. "Lemme look at you," he said. Then he hugged her, "Baby, I'm sure glad to see you."

"About time."

"Oh, baby, this is Billy Joe Tucker. I call him Red. We used to run together back in Moscow. I know you seed him a time or two with me." Nicholas said, as his drunken friend rose from the bench. The two exchanged acknowledging nods. Nicholas sensed the awkwardness of how Natasha found them. "Let's go," he said as he picked up Natasha's suitcase. "We'll stop and get you some breakfast."

"How was that long damn trip?" Billy Joe asked in a slow drawl as they walked outside and approached the truck.

"Horrible." Natasha said honestly. "Y'all look like y'all could use some breakfast too, she said as Nicholas put her suitcase in the back of the pick-up truck. Natasha looked at Nicholas intensely. He was as thin as always. He didn't seem changed at all. She had seen him on other occasions after he had too much to drink. His blue eyes were reddened; his thin face look strained and a familiar melancholy hovered about his aura like a Southern ghost. Billy Joe wore a beard and looked well fed. Natasha remembered seeing him with Nicholas on a few occasions back in Moscow, but his face was clean then and he didn't have as much weight. Billy Joe sat on the driver's side. Nicholas helped Natasha up and he climbed in behind her. Billy Joe started the truck up and drove off.

"Baby," Nicholas said, his arm around Natasha, "we didn't want to take a chance on being late, so we never went home last night. We had a few drinks at the club and when we left there, we came straight to the bus depot."

"Yeah, we had a few alright," Billy Joe said, "a few hundred."

"We got to the depot since three o'clock. That was better than going home and over-sleeping which I knowed would'a happened. We fell asleep in the truck outside the depot, and when they opened up this morning we went in and fell asleep again. We might not been awake when your bus got in, but we was there. Baby, I love you."

"I love you too Nicky."

Nicholas' breath emitted an unpleasant odor, but Natasha kissed him anyway. In fact, the smell of stale whiskey and beer had engulfed the cab of the truck. Natasha laid her head on Nicholas' shoulder and closed her eyes. For the first time since her mother paid a neighbor to drive her the sixty miles to Martinsburg to catch the bus, Natasha felt safe and sleepy. Now she could close her eyes and ride off into her future life in Charleston with hope and optimism. As soon as she dosed off to sleep, the truck slowed down and Billy Joe pulled into a parking spot at the restaurant.

Billy Joe locked the suitcase in the cab of truck, and then he and Nicholas walked Natasha to a table in the McDonald's restaurant. Then they went to the counter to order. "What you want?" Nicholas shouted back to the table where Natasha sat.

"A hammmburger." Natasha shouted back in an Appalachian accent that put most of the emphasis on the first syllable.

"Baby, they ain't serving hamburgers yet."

"Well that's what I want."

"Can you make up a few hamburgers?" Nicholas quietly asked the young black order taker.

"Not until eleven o'clock." The woman said bluntly. Then she pointed to the breakfast menu on the wall. "Can I take your orders?" she said.

Billy Joe ordered three sausage and egg biscuits, three home fries, juice and coffee.

"Baby, they ain't serving hamburgers until after eleven. Lemme get you something else? Sausage and eggs, bacon and eggs, ham and eggs, home fries, apple pie?" Nicholas read from the wall menu.

"Whatever," Natasha said. Perhaps it was the result of the long bus ride but this attitude was completely out of character for her.

In two minutes, Nicholas and Billy Joe returned to their table. Nicholas lowered his tray. It held six mixed biscuit sandwiches, apple pie, juice, and coffee. They ate in between inquiries about the people back in Moscow. Sleep was overtaking Natasha. Her answers got to be slow and her voice began to drag. She stopped eating and yawned. "I gotta go to sleep," she said.

"What you need is a drink," Nicholas said as he signaled Billy Joe to gather up the uneaten food. Nicholas walked Natasha to the truck while Billy Joe got a box to put the food in. Then they all loaded into the truck and drove off toward the apartment house. During the drive, Nicholas reached under the seat to get a vodka bottle that still had a good drink left in it. He gave it to Natasha and she drank it right from the bottle and fell right off to sleep.

The Fairview Manor is a run down sub-division in a poor section of the renegade city of North Charleston. The city had just recently split from the peninsular city of Charleston. The tenants are half-transitory indigents on their way to a better job, a home of their own, carfare to another state, or, deeper into despair and the bottle. The other half of the tenants are composed of native black Charlestonians, many of them stuck right there between the *rock* and the hard place, a sprinkling of Mexicans and two or three groups of Filipinos. In 1979, this was an uneasy mix of people. There were tensions, suspicions, distrust, and antagonism. People in the real estate business realized that integration was here to stay and that on this social and economic level, there was money to be made experimenting with it.

This was a neighborhood of drugs and thievery, but the apartments were fully occupied because through diligence or a job, the rent was affordable. And, although these people aren't far different economically and sociably from the people Natasha knew in Moscow, what would be new to her is the diversity of poverty. Nicholas didn't mention any of this in his letters. Nor did he mention the fact that he was sharing a three-bedroom apartment with a large group of people, the numbers changed constantly, but it was seldom under nine and at times as high as fifteen. People moved in and out, as their personal needs dictated. This apartment served as a gateway to a better life for some as they acquired permanent jobs and moved on into the general society. "The House" as they referred to the apartment, also served as a lifeline for those down on their luck, a place where one washed, ate, and slept. Those who couldn't find steady work maintained those privileges at the house for a reasonable period of time. And, if you were thought to be sincere in your efforts to find work, the more fortunate ones shared the after work beers, whiskey, and reefers with you. Those who were found to be slackers were driven off. These unwritten protocols were never discussed; they just developed over time. Down at the bottom of the bottom there is charity, but no room for deadbeats.

Everyone was asleep in the house. It seemed every inch of space was occupied. People slept in sleeping bags on the floor. A young woman slept on a sofa in what could have been the living room. A television was on the floor under a window. A shadeless floor lamp stood in a corner. The rooms had very little furniture. The kitchen was small and dirty. The air was stale with cigarette smoke. Natasha was tired and sleepy. She knew she wasn't dreaming, but this all had the feel of an exciting dream of exploration. Nicholas led her to one of the bedrooms and Billy Joe followed. There was a young woman asleep on a mattress on the floor. "Hey Brenda. Brenda." Billy Joe called out bending over the woman. The woman arose and after what was for her, a hazy introduction, left the bedroom with Billy Joe. Nicholas put the suitcase in a corner and closed the bedroom door.

"You wanna take a shower before you sleep?" he asked.

"I just wanna sleep," Natasha said and began to undress.

"This is gonna be our room. You and me, and Billy Joe and Brenda."

"Well why they just leave?"

"You know," Nicholas said, undressing.

When Nicholas and Natasha awoke it was three in the afternoon. The people in the house had all long been awake and were well into their Saturday routine. The house had a fenced-in medium sized back yard. Most of the house crew lounged around in the yard drinking beer and listening to vintage rock and roll on the radio. Nicholas and Natasha showered, dressed, and arrived in the yard with big smiles. Nicholas introduced Natasha to everyone. Billy Joe and Brenda came over and gave them cups and a beer each. They all sat on the grass by the wall where there should have been flowers. Then a fifth size bottle of vodka was passed to the new arrivals to the yard. Natasha poured a drink and drank it down in a manner that showed familiarity with the process. Elizabeth, a young woman who is called Beth and who lived in the house with her husband Stanley Wells, made a celebratory shout. "Go on honey. You one of us now," Beth then said. Beth rose, walked over to Natasha and kissed her on the cheek. The talk turned into a playful tease of Nicholas as a traditional welcoming of his mate to the tribe. There was lots of laughter and drinking. Then someone arrived with two buckets of fried chicken, corn-on-the-cob, and dirty rice. The food was put on a table by the door. Natasha was encouraged to be the first one to fix a plate. She was having the time of her life and she hadn't been in

Charleston for a full day yet. And, there was so much more to anticipate. She thought about how she would show Nicholas her appreciation when they returned to bed, but right now it was time to party. The merry-making went on until the early morning for most of the crew, but Natasha and Nicholas went back to bed around midnight.

Natasha's first weeks in Charleston were filled with days that excited her despite their similarity. Some of the people at the house were in between jobs; a few of the women, who were married or attached to a guy, didn't work at all. So each day, there was a different assortment of people at the house with idle time. Each day she went to the malls with a different combination of her new roommates. They walked the malls, looked at the merchandise in the shops, and daydreamed about the time when they could afford to own these things. When they returned home, they would have a few beers. In the evenings when the workers returned, the real drinking began as they arranged to buy dinners of pizza, or chicken, or burgers. Food was heated and reheated, but very little food was ever cooked there. They would get drunk in the yard and one by one ease off to a spot to sleep. The newness of it all made Natasha bubble with excitement. She stayed up all night and was always one of the last to go to bed. Although Billy Joe and Brenda slept on a mattress next to them, when Natasha got to bed, she would wake Nicky and she would insist they make love. Because her reality was distorted by beer, whiskey, and reefer, on these late night episodes, she thought this was done in quiet and secrecy, but there were times when Billy Joe and Brenda heard them and became aroused themselves and they would make love also.

On the weekends, Nicholas and Natasha would go to the beach with small groups, or go walking the streets of downtown Charleston. The beach was fun, but Natasha didn't feel comfortable in a bathing suit, so sometimes she would make up other excuses to get out of going. Natasha loved everything about Charleston, the rich look of its homes, its grand Southern charm, streets so clean she felt guilty dropping a cigarette butt on them. And, the bars crowded with sophisticated young people who acted like royalty. Natasha studied these people intensely; she was impressed by their highborn behavior. In all of her life in Moscow, she never came across a single person who displayed such regal bearings. These young people in the bars and cafes of Charleston emitted the sense that they ruled the world. Their teeth were white and straight, their faces and bodies were tan, and their eyes were bright with unlimited possibilities. Some of these young people were Charleston Bluebloods, but most of them were from the educated middle-class. Natasha thought these people had a certain dignity about them even when they were drunk and boisterous; they did everything with sophistication.

These people were everything she was not, everything her ancestry was not, everything Nicholas was not. She came from a town of rednecks. She was a redneck, Nicholas was a redneck, so was everyone at the house. They all came from a social class that was scorned and belittled. These other people had everything she wanted for herself and for Nicky. It depressed her that she did not know how she would get there, but she knew instinctively that she would work to better her conditions and die trying if need be. After all, she was young, and Nicky was young, and this was America where all things were possible; even the prospects of a backwoods girl like her obtaining the success that creates that air of superiority she admired in those young people she saw in the bars of Charleston. Natasha never once discussed this with Nicholas during the summer.

Time fled by fast and the week that Natasha was to return to Moscow was near. Over the summer, Brenda and Natasha became good friends, not only because of the closeness of their boyfriends, but also, because they genuinely liked each other. It was a Friday evening and Brenda had planned a girl's night out to a party given by the husband of a girl who once worked with her. Natasha, Brenda, and Beth would be going and they had all discussed this with their men, who made plans of their own for the evening. Billy Joe even left the pick-up truck for Brenda to drive. That evening the girls piled into the truck, lit up two joints and drove off. They passed the marijuana cigarettes between each other until they burned their fingers.

"Girl, you going back to West Virginia next week." Brenda said to Natasha, who sat on the other side of Beth, near the other window.

"Yeah, you know, we're going to miss you." Beth said.

"Poor Nicholas, I ain't never seed him so happy until you came," Brenda said. "He really loves you."

"I know he loves me," Natasha said, somewhat agitated that the subject was brought up. She had been thinking about her predicament for a week now and hadn't come up with a way to approach her mother with the idea of her staying in South Carolina indefinitely. She had only sent two brief letters to her mother over the summer and had received two brief letters in return. Although she was sure of Nicholas' love, there was, in her mind, still the question of whether Nicholas really wanted her to stay. How much would he do, how far would he go to keep her here? He had not tried to influence her one way or the other, in fact, her returning to Moscow never came up for discussion.

"And you love him too, don't you?" Beth asked.

"He's the only man ever for me," Natasha said, "I just ain't made up my mind about what to do yet."

"Like she got all the time in the world. Look girl, if where you come from anything like where I come from, there ain't no choice to be made. My little small town in Arkansas ain't got shit—not even a post office," Brenda said.

"Oh, don't get me wrong," Natasha said, "I like it here and I want to stay, but…."

"But what?" Beth asked.

"I wan'ta be married.

"Married!" Brenda and Beth laughed. They thought this was the sentiment of a silly young girl.

"That ain't nothing but a piece of paper, you got the man—be satisfied," Brenda said.

Beth was married and had a respect for the institution of Holy Union. She disagreed with Brenda. "I'm not saying that Nicholas would ever dump you. I think he loves you very much, but it would be a lot harder for him to ever dump you if you were married," Beth said.

"It's not about any of that," Natasha said.

"For me the thing is this," Beth said, "I can't see how you can expect him to marry you after six short weeks of playing house."

"Six weeks," Natasha screamed out. "Six weeks my ass, we been together for four years."

"How old are you?" Beth asked.

"Eighteen," Natasha said. "I'll be nineteen in September."

"And he's been having sex with you since you were fourteen—that shit's against the law. I like doing it, but even I didn't start until I was twenty," Beth said with a grin.

"Stop lying Elizabeth," Brenda said in a motherly tone.

"Okay, nineteen," Beth said.

"Elizabeth?"

"Okay, seventeen, and that's the truth."

They all broke into a laugh and lit up cigarettes to compliment the marijuana now talking effect. The party was being held at a house in the country. The effect of the marijuana gave the girls an acute awareness of the countryside as they drove.

"What's your folks gonna say if you stay?" Brenda asked.

"I don't know. It's just my momma, my daddy been done run off. She wants me to come back to attend community college. I want to go to college, but I want to stay here. I want to be on my own and get a job, and marry Nicky, and have a house, and children, and a van, and a truck and a swimming pool, two dogs, and an attitude like them bitches in Charleston."

"You ain't pregnant are you girl? Brenda asked.

"Hell no. It ain't nothing like that."

"Think what would happen if you were?" Beth said. Your momma wouldn't want you back with her with another mouth to feed. Nicholas would have to marry you, or, at least, support you and the child."

"If you ain't pregnant, don't get pregnant," Brenda said. "You too young for all that headache. Just call your momma and tell her you're staying. What she gonna do—come get you?"

"It's not so much my momma, as it is what Nicky wants."

"He wants you—we all know that," Beth said, as Brenda drove the truck up to the house. The front yard was crowded with cars, trucks, and a few motorcycles.

Brenda parked the truck and they all got out and walked around the house to the backyard. The backyard was crowded with people drinking, eating and having loud conversations. Loud country music was blaring from a country and western station on the radio. One group of men, beers in their hands, stood by a grill cooking hamburgers and hot dogs. Another group stood by a grill turning steaks. Coolers, filled with beer were everywhere. There was a table near the door to the family room that held liquor, plates, cups, and large bowls of salads. Out near the fence was a brick grill pit that held a golden crisp hundred and fifty pound hog that had been cooked to near perfection. Brenda maneuvered the girls through the crowd saying hello to people they passed and quickly found Cathy, the girl who with her husband were hosting the party. Brenda introduced her friends to Cathy and asked about her husband. Cathy offered them a drink and after they had gotten beers, she took them around to introduce them to her friends and to Dave, her husband, who was now putting the finishing touches to the hog. Natasha and Beth settled in with a group and Brenda went off with Cathy. This was around nine o'clock and it had gotten dark. Natasha and Beth moved separately from group to group and they both saw Cathy many times during the evening, but it wasn't until the party was breaking up that they saw Brenda again.

"Where in the fuck you been all night?" Beth asked Brenda as they drove back home.

"At the party," Brenda said. "That was some good damn hog."

"It was," Natasha said, "but how would you know, you wasn't there to get any."

"That was some gooood damn hog," Brenda said, and the girls drove home in near silence. They got back home at three in the morning to empty beds.

Natasha awoke at ten o'clock. Brenda and Billy Joe had already gotten up and gone with a group to Shoney's for breakfast. Nicholas was asleep and snoring. Natasha pushed his shoulder gently.

"Nicky, Nicky." There was no response. "Nicholas wake up, we gotta talk." Then she shook his head.

"Whaaat, what you want," Nicholas said, his eyes still closed.

"I want to talk to you."

"I got home right after you. You was sleeping so I didn't wake you up. Now go back to sleep; we'll talk in the morning."

"It's morning now and I really want to talk to you."

Nicholas' eyes popped open. "Oh shit, what time is it? I was supposed to work some overtime today."

"I don't know, but it should be about eleven."

"I gotta go baby. We're wiring this house that gotta be finished by Monday. I really gotta go. We'll talk this evening, I promise."

"Nicholas," Natasha screamed as Nicholas rose and went to the bathroom.

Saturday's mail brought Natasha a letter from her mother. Natasha was hesitant about opening the letter afraid that it would bear instructions for returning home. Instead, the letter carried a pleasant tone with a tale or two of how well her siblings were doing and the number of the family's first ever telephone. In the letter, Natasha's mother asked that she call, but said nothing about her return. Natasha read the letter two times to be sure that it didn't say it was time to come home. Natasha had made up her mind; she was staying in Charleston. After she had her talk with Nicholas, she would call her mother on the new telephone to explain her decision. That Saturday evening when Nicholas returned from work, Natasha was the only one still at the house. She had resisted several invitations out to the local haunts in the hope that she would get this chance to talk with Nicholas alone. Her return ticket to Moscow was for Wednesday, August fourteenth, four days away. Nicholas opened a beer and they walked out to the back yard. They avoided two shaky chairs and sat on the ground.

"Now-what's going on?" Nicholas asked.

"I got a letter from momma today," Natasha said.

"What'd it say?"

"You know I go back on Wednesday," Natasha said, dodging a direct answer in an attempt to imply that the letter referred to her return.

"You're suppose to."

"We ain't talked about that," Natasha said tearfully. "You ain't said nothing about it."

"Well what you gonna do?"

"What you want me to do?"

"I want you to do what's gonna make you happy, baby. You did promise your momma about going to that community college."

"Then you want me to go back?"

"I love you baby."

"But, you want me to go back?"

"I love you baby."

"Nicholas."

Nicholas reached into his pocket and pulled out a small box. He opened the box and in it was an inexpensive cut diamond ring that stopped Natasha's heart—it might as well have been the Hope Diamond. She was speechless, it was as though Nicholas had read her mind, or perhaps, their two minds had merged as one.

"What's this?" Natasha asked when she regained her senses.

"Baby, would you marry me?" Nicholas asked as he removed the ring from the box and offered it up for Natasha's finger and future.

"Nicky, Nicky," Natasha said as she guided her finger through the ring. She embraced Nicholas and sobbed uncontrollably.

On Wednesday, the day she was to return to Moscow, Natasha telephoned her mother and told her that she and Nicholas were getting married that coming Saturday. To Natasha's surprise, her mother offered no resistance. She only cautioned Natasha to be certain she was doing the right thing and reminded her that she should continue her education. Natasha had dreaded making what turned out to be a very easy phone conversation. At noon on Saturday, Nicholas Hilgrown and Natasha White were married in the back yard, by a preacher from a local church. The reception, which started even before the wedding, went on through out the night. Natasha received many comments of congratulations from the people at the wedding and snarl looks from Brenda. Nicholas and Natasha finally left the wedding party to spend the rest of the night in a local hotel. Natasha Hilgrown awoke early Sunday morning, her head filled with plans; Nicholas needed a truck, she would get a job, they would move to a place of their own. She knew that Nicholas loved her deeply, but he had no vision for their future. It would be her role to plan out their destiny. Back in her subconscious lay a deep confusion about the looks that she had been receiving from Brenda since her announcement. Brenda didn't care for marriage or work; Natasha was determined to do both. Natasha didn't know what this meant for their relationship, but she was determine to handle whatever Brenda threw her way. Nothing would stand between her, Nicholas, and their happiness.

On Monday morning, Natasha had Beth drive her to the mall to fill out job applications. She filled out applications at three stores before she was hired on the spot at Regal's

Department Store in North Charleston, a mile from the Fairway Manor. She was hired as a sales clerk and was asked to come in the next morning to begin three days of training. She would start working on the sales floor on Friday. Natasha was bloated with pride the entire day. She drank beer and practiced how she would break the news to Nicholas. He would soon be getting his electrician's license and with her extra salary, they could save enough money to get a place of their own. All day long, her mind raced through a mix of scenarios. Nicholas needed his own truck and she would need a car to get to work, but for now she would walk the mile when she couldn't get someone to drive her there and someone to pick her up. She felt strong and in control of things. Just a few weeks from nineteen and life was going to be beautiful.

That evening when Natasha broke the news to Nicholas, his reaction surprised her. He seemed indifferent, almost disappointed.

"Now what'd you go and do that for?" he asked.

"So we can get out of here and be on our own."

"I thought you like it here?"

"Nicky, it's a good place to get a start from, but we're not back in Moscow, we're in a place where we can move ahead and make a good life for ourselves."

"You're not having fun here?"

"Yeah, I'm having fun, but we're married now and we'll have more fun in our own place."

After that conversation, Nicholas was completely helpful in making arrangements for someone to take Natasha to work and someone to pick her up. Her starting hours rotated from morning to afternoon and this made it difficult to always get a ride. Sometimes, she had to walk to work. Her major concern was that on the two nights a week that she got off at nine o'clock she would be picked up. Nicholas was always able to borrow a vehicle to make the quick trip to the store and back. Natasha's having a job strained her relationship with Brenda. On Natasha's day's off from work, Brenda always found a reason to avoid her company. Brenda didn't even stay at the celebration party they held when Nicholas received his electrician's license because the party was also for Natasha's nineteenth birthday. She had one drink and remembered that Cathy had invited her out to her place. Brenda liked Natasha, but she didn't like Natasha's eagerness to change things, more specifically, she didn't like Natasha's method of changing things by working. Brenda had her own ambitions to get ahead, but working wasn't in her plan, not while she remained a woman, and men existed.

Natasha got to know her work and loved working with her customers. Regal's Department store sold quality merchandise that drew middle-class customers whose mannerisms Natasha gauged, studied, and filed away for future review. She made friends with some of the other girls who worked with her. They, too, were different than the girls at the house, or her companions back in Moscow. These girls went to college in one form or another. Some of them spoke about becoming managers at the store. They were up-beat, progressive people with positive goals and positive plans for reaching their goals. Natasha mentioned all of this in her few letters to her family back home. In a few weeks, Natasha became particularly close to a girl named Nina Gold. Nina was eight years older than Natasha, but Natasha had matured so much over the summer that Nina accepted her as an equal. They ate lunch together when their schedule permitted and on payday, they went out for drinks. Sometimes when they had the same day off from work, Nina would pick Natasha up and they would spend the day at Nina's boyfriend's house in Summerville. This further alienated Brenda and even Beth felt slighted by Natasha's new freedom.

Natasha opened a bank account with her first paycheck. Each week, she deposited her entire paycheck and she got Nicholas to save some of his money in the account. In eight weeks, she made a sizable withdrawal of their savings. That Saturday morning, Natasha walked with Nicholas to a near by used car lot where he picked out a blue, 1975, Toyota pick-up truck with seventy-five thousand miles on the odometer. She paid for the truck with cash and Nicholas smilingly drove her to work. When she got off from work at nine o'clock that night, Nicholas waited in the parking lot to pick her up with a six pack of beer. "There's my husband over there in the blue truck," Natasha said to a girl who worked with her. "See you tomorrow, " Natasha said, her pride showing as she dashed off towards the truck. Nicholas kissed her, handed her a beer, and drove off. "You did good," he said. "You did real good."

Natasha continued to save and now the goal was an apartment of their own. She knew how attached Nicholas and Billy Joe were, so she came up with a scheme to use their closeness to enhance her ability to continue to save and pay the rent for an apartment. They would take Billy Joe and Brenda with them and share the rent. Natasha discussed her plan with Nicholas and he seemed pleased that she had included Billy Joe and Brenda in their future in an intimate way. Natasha knew that Brenda would object, but her options were few, she would have to go along and, maybe, even get herself a job. Natasha did everything herself. She scanned the newspaper daily looking for an apartment. All the listings in the paper were for more money than she wanted to pay. She didn't want a really good place; right now; just something that would get them away from the house crowd, and still allow them to save toward her next goal—a home.

Natasha had mentioned to her associates on the job that she was looking for an apartment. One night right before closing time, a woman from another department who heard about Natasha's search for an apartment, told her about a trailer she owned and wanted to rent out. The trailer was in a development just a few blocks from the store. It had two tiny bedrooms, a kitchen and a living room and the rent was minimal. This wasn't what Natasha had in mind, she detested the stigma attached to living in a trailer, but everything else was right. This could very well be a blessing. Natasha told Nicholas that they were moving. She told him to inform Billy Joe to have half the rent money. There was no lease to sign and no security money to put up. The next week, over Brenda's protest, the two couples moved into the trailer. Brenda didn't speak to Natasha all of the first week, but life in the trailer soon settled into a routine.

Old habits persist. The couples still spent much of their time at the house with the people they once lived with. Most evenings they went there straight from work and sometimes stayed over night. This prompted the question: "Why'd ya move?" and the taunt "Go home...please." The house was still the place that held the excitement of drinking and enjoyable conversations for Nicholas and Billy Joe. And, there was always the melodrama of who would show up and with what for the head? Natasha went mostly because Nicholas would be there. For Brenda it was home. The trailer was used as a place to store their few personal possessions and as a place to sleep.

One day Natasha and her co-worker, Nina, went to the trailer to have lunch. There they could drink a couple of beers with their lunch. When Natasha opened the door to the trailer, the smell and the sound hit them immediately and simultaneously. There were people in the bedroom used by Billy Joe and Brenda having loud sex. They heard the walloping beat of the bed and the accompanying moans and groans. Natasha moved towards the room without thinking and Nina followed. It wasn't until she reached the door that a tidbit of fear about who might be in there entered her mind. Natasha pushed the door open, Nina followed so closely her body pushed Natasha into the room. The woman sat on top of the man, her legs bent back. She bounced up and down and waved her arm in the air like riding a bronco. The man lay flat and submissive, moving his head from side to side like he had been conquered. Nina let out a giggle. The naked and startled pair turned their heads toward the door and stopped their movements. It was Brenda; a strange look of anger in her eyes and ecstasy on her face, biting down on her bottom lip. The man beneath her was Cathy's husband Dave; his expression was purely that of surprise. Dave's arms dropped to either side of the tiny bed as a pleading look took over his face. Nothing was said verbally, volumes of emotions streamed thought the air as all the eyes met for a moment. Natasha turned and pushed Nina back toward the kitchen. There they paused for a second, then left through the kitchen door, slamming it shut.

"That bitch," Natasha said.

"She was *doing* that dude," Nina said laughing. "Ringing his motherfucking gongs."

"That bitch," Natasha repeated. "While we all out working to pay the rent that bitch is fucking some dipstick in our home. Cheating on Billy Joe with her friend's husband. How low can that bitch get?"

"Who's the dude?" Nina asked.

"A dipstick named Dave something, I don't know his last

name. But he is married to a girl name Cathy from Summerville. Cathy and that bitch in there are supposed to be good friends. You know I remember going to a party with Brenda and Beth out at Cathy's and Dave's house. Brenda disappeared for the whole evening and now that I think of it, I didn't see Dave for most of the evening either. She's a whore, a stinking no good whore and I gotta get her ass outta my house."

"What are you gonna do?"

"I don't know. I'm gonna tell Nicholas about this shit. One way or another—that bitch has gotta go. Billy Joe works to support the whore, gives her money and buys her food and other things and look what she done."

"Well one thing for sure," Nina said, "that girl can take care of business. She was riding that dude—whipping it on him."

"Oh come on girl, we just got enough time left to get a burger and get back to work on time."

"No, really," Nina said, as they walked back towards the mall, "I like her technique."

That evening Natasha convinced Nicholas to leave the house and go home to the trailer early. She was still agitated enough by Brenda's behavior that Nicholas could sense that something was upsetting her. When they arrived at the trailer, the door was unlocked. Natasha sat Nicholas down, opened two beers, and began to explain what she had witnessed that day. She told Nicholas about Brenda's disappearance at the party at Cathy's house. Then she threw in some speculation about unknown others. Nicholas showed no surprise after hearing about the day's event. In fact, he behaved as if he knew about Brenda's unfaithfulness all the time and he kind of hinted that Billy Joe suspected it also. Nicholas promised that he would speak to Billy Joe about the whole thing. He told Natasha that he was sure that Billy Joe would dump Brenda because she didn't mean anything to him. In Nicholas' assessment, it was a relationship of convenience. Billy Joe had a cheating woman who could only break his heart by drinking his last beer. Natasha took Nicholas back to the bedroom where the act took place and there they discovered Brenda's intentions when they saw that the room was trashed and most of Brenda's things were gone.

Nicholas Hilgrown and Billy Joe Tucker had known each other all their lives. They grew up in houses less then a mile from each other's. They both came from poor Moscow families. Billy Joe saw little of his father who traveled from out of state job to out of state job. He had five brothers, one sister, and a frail mother. They lived on the little money the father sent home intermittently and what money the older boys could scrape together. Nicholas had two brothers and a mother who was strong in Christian faith. His father died from the over use of liquor, when Nicholas was still a young boy. Alcoholism had been a problem so endemic in Moscow that it seems it was transmitted through the genes or communicable by physical contact. The fact is, drinking gave the entire male population, and in the younger generations, the female population, the means to eliminate the dullness of existing in the shadows of the living. The town's alcoholic epidemic was created by decades of hopelessness and was as dangerous as a loaded shotgun. Alcoholism was contagious in Moscow's cultural environment. The younger people's preference for narcotics loaded the other barrel of despair in Moscow County. This is the atmosphere young Nicholas Hilgrown and Billy Joe Tucker knew in their formative years. Alcoholic and absent fathers, idle adults, dire poverty, a cultural vacuum, and a subordinate locality are the materials the youth of Moscow had to mold their lives.

Nicholas and Billy Joe were just months apart in age. They played together since first grade and learned to depend on each other even more so than their own brothers. In the summer, the sun would turn Billy Joe's skin deep red. Nicholas began affectionately referring to him as Red. By the time the boys were ten years old, they were street scamps providing for their own daily distractions and nourishment. There was no one in the school system who was accountable for the attendance of students, so they sporadically attended school. They took their first drinks during this time, but didn't become weekend drinkers until they were thirteen, when they were also introduced to marijuana. The two boys protected each other in school and on the streets and were inseparable throughout high school. Nicholas and Billy Joe attended a trade school that prepared students to become electricians, carpenters, and plumbers. They selected the electrical course and were genuinely involved in learning the trade. The school had an arrangement with developers in other counties that allowed the boys to gain experience in their trade working for sub-contractors on homes that were being built by the developers. The school was paid a small sum by the developers, who also bought supplies for the school. The developers saved thousands of dollars in free labor on each home. The boys were exploited for the last two years of high school. They didn't get paid nor did they receive any health insurance or other employment benefits, but they loved the feel of going to work rather than school and didn't think of themselves as being abused. Nicholas and Billy Joe had gone through all of this together and they developed an unbreakable bond.

After they finished high school they continued to work for the sub-contractor, but the work was unsteady and the pay was substandard. They were promised apprenticeship positions that would lead to obtaining their electrician licenses, but in three years that never happened. Each time they asked about it, they were told that they hadn't accumulated enough hours to be enrolled in the apprenticeship program. Finally, in disgust Billy Joe followed another buddy to Charleston, South Carolina. Billy Joe tried desperately to convince Nicholas to come with him, but Nicholas resisted. The Charleston area was going through a major change. Integration and the relaxation of racial tensions brought growth and prosperity to many areas of Charleston County as many national companies expanded into the South. There were lots of jobs with home constructing sub-contractors and the pay was better than they received at home, but there was still no health insurance, sick pay, or other benefits. After a few letters from Billy Joe, Nicholas, still out of work, packed up and followed.

"So when will you tell him?" Natasha asked.

"When he gets in, if he ain't too drunk, or, maybe tomorrow. You can be here when I talk to him, but I don't want you to say anything—okay?"

"Okay?"

"Okay. You want to go back to the house?"

"No. Let's go to bed."

"Okay, but let me go get a bottle first?"

"Okay."

Nicholas and Natasha were having their first drink from the new bottle when Billy Joe came home. Nicholas poured him a drink.

"Sit down Red." Nicholas said.

"Oh, oh," Billy Joe mumbled. He knew that when Nicholas called him Red he was summoning up the sacredness of their relationship from their days in Moscow.

They were all seated around the small kitchen table.

Natasha sat with her head on the table like she wasn't even there.

"Look, I gotta tell this to you. We have been together all our life. We're brother's man."

Billy Joe's face was blank. He was ready to hear the worse. He took a drink and looked straight at Nicholas.

"Natasha and her friend Nina popped in on Brenda and some dude back in your room today. Fucking."

Nicholas' bluntness snapped Natasha's head up. She gave Nicholas a stern look, while carefully avoiding Billy Joe's eyes. She didn't want to project any sentiment and she didn't want to see whatever emotions Billy Joe let escape.

"There just ain't no other way for me to say it," Nicholas continued. "We have known each other too long not to be able to say it like it is. Look Red, you know Brenda wasn't right all along. I know you knowed it. Well the shit hit the fan today. I don't think you need to worry about getting rid of the bitch— looks like her clothes are gone."

Although Natasha didn't want to exchange visual sentiments with Billy Joe, her ears were keenly awaiting his words. She didn't know what words to expect, but he would have to say something.

"You alright, Red?" Nicholas asked.

"Man I thought you had bad news from home or something," Billy Joe said, convincingly masking his disappointment and embarrassment. Billy Joe finished his drink. "I'm going to bed now."

When Billy Joe got back to his room, he screamed out "Aaaaah shit."

"You alright, Red?" Nicholas asked. "You alright man?"

"What-in-the-fuck happened to my room?"

The three Moscow refuges lived together in the trailer

for two years before Natasha saved up enough money to start looking for a small house. Their routine had haltered only in small ways. They still met up at the house several evenings a week for lots of drinking and marijuana smoking. They got along with Billy Joe like he was family. They took care of each other and were totally honest with each other. The change was that through her job at Regals, Natasha met people that enlarged their circle of friends. And, every so often, she was able to get Nicholas and Billy Joe to a party with a different group of folks. Even as their circle of friends grew larger, it seemed to Natasha, that her world grew smaller. She wrote to her mother less and less. Once in a while, she would receive a letter from her sister, in which she was told mom said hello. They seldom went to the beach during the summer months and visits to Charleston bars were even less frequent. Natasha's admiration of that crowd had dimmed, not because she no longer revered them, she still did, but it just wasn't who she was discovering herself to be. A certain degree of self-acceptance hovered beneath the surface of her consciousness.

The people at the house were in a state of constant change. Beth and Stanley Wells had a baby and moved to an apartment in Summerville. The gossip was that Brenda had gone to Las Vegas on a motorcycle with a carpenter to become a showgirl. Brenda didn't find any work as a showgirl because although she was good looking and had a sexy figure, she didn't have any talent in dancing, singing or acting. In time, the carpenter moved on to California. Brenda stayed put and as the gossip goes, using her one real talent, she had become a popular and successful attraction at a bordello called The Dude Ranch. Nearly all of the people at the house now are recent arrivals. The alumni are spread out all over a three county area, but many still came back to the house, although less and less frequently.

An event that brought most of the former housemates back was the death of Christopher Stevens, the first guy to bring in a boarder and start the whole tradition. He died in an automobile accident coming home early on a Sunday morning. Christopher was from Tupelo, Mississippi. Current and former housemates all contributed to a fund to have Christopher's body sent back home for burial. A small group of his friends even accompanied the body back to Mississippi. Nicholas and Billy Joe were among them. They were gone for three days.

This was the first time Nicholas and Natasha had been separated for longer then a day since she first arrived in Charleston. Natasha didn't visit the house all the time Nicholas was gone, instead, after work she went home. She used this time alone to take stock. She reflected on all of the events of her life, past and present. Where she was and where she was headed. She was making progress; living *her* version of the American Dream. She was particularly happy with the strength of her relationship with Nicholas. She was absolutely sure of his love and loyalty. And, she was sure that she loved him even more than ever. It was during this process that Natasha came to grips with the fact that she hadn't had a period in two months. With more time by herself, and less distractions, it became impossible for Natasha to continue to ignore what was going on with her body. Natasha had been using birth control pills since she became sexually active back in Moscow, but since she married, she became more reckless. There were many times during many months when she had skipped taking a dosage. Until now, there had been no consequences. She didn't find the possibility of an impending pregnancy disturbing since they would purchase a house before the baby arrived, she simply hadn't set aside the time to consider it. Even before Natasha had fully explored and reconciled her own feeling about having a baby, she found herself wondering what Nicholas' feeling would be and how he would take the news. They had discussed having children, but only in vague talks about an abstract future. The future, sometimes, has a way of arriving crystal-clear and uninvited. Natasha decided to go to the free clinic in Summerville on her next day off from work.

Nicholas and Billy Joe had been back for several days and Natasha said nothing to Nicholas about her suspicion, nor had she gone to the free clinic on her day off. On the days that she was off, she used any distraction to avoid thinking about going to the clinic. She took clothes to the laundry to wash. She ironed Nicholas' work clothes. She dusted and straightened up the trailer. When she knew that the clinic was closed, she drank a six pack of beer. Her behavior was cold and odd. She stopped going to the house after work altogether. She went home to the trailer after work and prepared dinner such as it were. When Nicholas tried to ask her what was going on, she would cry and scold him for not coming home for dinner or for coming home late and drunk. In the mornings, she was tense and her face was flushed. She was continually agitated. After a week of being frustrated by Natasha's behavior, Nicholas asked her if she wanted to see a doctor. Natasha apathetically reminded him that they didn't have any health insurance and a doctor's visit would be too costly. The following week, Nicholas came directly home after work. He ate dinner with Natasha and joined Billy Joe and the others at the house after the evening's argument with Natasha.

At the end of the week, Nicholas thought he had figured it out. She wanted a more structured life. While driving around in North Charleston, he saw a "For Sale" sign on a small house. The house was in disrepair, but not beyond the restoration abilities of Nicholas and Billy Joe and, if necessary, they would enlist the help of some of their colleagues in the trades. Nicholas knew that Natasha had been saving every penny she could towards the purchase of their own home. Maybe if he showed some interest and made a move to get them into a home, she would snap out of her present bitchiness. Nicholas smiled a confident smile; he had figured it all out. He would make romance to Natasha with the news of this prospective house and a suitcase of beer. Natasha was off that day and would be home cooking dinner. Nicholas knew that Billy Joe went on to the house after work, so he and Natasha would have a chance to work this out alone. It was after six o'clock in the evening so Nicholas was surprised that Natasha was not home when he got there. There was no scent of cooked food. He opened a beer and put the others in the refrigerator. Nicholas turned the radio on and sat down at the kitchen table. He heard a car pull up next to the trailer. He looked out of the window. It was Nina's black Pontiac. Natasha got out and closed the door. She leaned through the downed window to talk to Nina. She pulled her head back and before she straightened up stuck her head back in the car. A minute later, she repeated the action. Nicholas could hardly see Nina's small figure, but her head bobbed in animation. Natasha finally pulled her head back and walked away from the car waving good bye as Nina drove away. Nicholas greeted Natasha at the door with an opened beer.

"Baby I've got good news," Nicholas said, as he led Natasha to a chair at the kitchen table. He took her pocketbook and threw it on the sofa by the television set.

"I got news too," Natasha said, taking a sip of beer. Then she went to the sofa to retrieve her pocketbook. She took out her cigarettes and lit one up while she sat. Her voice was matter-of-fact and Nicholas didn't know what to make of this tone.

"Go 'head hit me with it," he said.

"Well, you said you got good news. Let's hear your news first—'cause I really don't know if my news is good or bad."

"Where you been?"

"I'll tell you in a while. What you got to tell me that's so good?"

"That I bought a suitcase of beer and it's all in the fridge."

"Nicky stop the bullshit."

"No, baby, now go on tell me—where you been today. Now go on. I got a surprise for you, but you can't hear it until you tell me your news. That was Nina you was with right? Where'd she take you?"

Natasha never could resist the word *surprise* so for her the game was over.

"Nicky, I had her take me to..." Natasha took a deep breath. "Nina went with me to the clinic."

"To the clinic? Baby you alright?"

"I'm fine."

"Did you see a doctor?"

"Yeah, I saw a doctor. I took some testes."

"So what did the doctor say?"

"He said I'm pregnant," Natasha said, rushing the words out so fast that all Nicholas heard was "NANT."

"What?"

"I'm gonna have a baby. I'm pregnant."

Nicholas stared at Natasha for what, to her, seemed like an eternity, his mouth opened, his face aghast. He was truly speechless. He tried to speak, but no words came forth. He stood up from his chair and kneeled down before her, his arms resting on her thighs, his head in her lap. His gesture was so profound it filled her with emotion. She placed a hand on his head and rubbed it. He looked up at her and his eyes were filled with tears. His body began to shake. Natasha rubbed and patted his back. Then she leaned her body over enveloping his head. They silently held each other in that position for an hour.

"Nicky," Natasha said softly, trying not to break the mood, "what's your feelings."

"Feelings about what?"

"You know."

"Baby, I'm the happiest man in the world."

Nicholas looked in Natasha's eyes earnestly and she knew that what he said was true. She kissed his head. He raised himself up from the floor and gave her an emotional and passionate kiss. Then he patted her stomach with one hand and took a cigarette from her pack with the other. He walked to the refrigerator and opened two beers.

"What else did the doctor say?" Nicholas asked as he lit the cigarette.

"Well, that I'm maybe ten weeks gone. That I need to start seeing a doctor regular and things like that."

"What about him?"

"Nicholas, I went to the free clinic. The doctor's there volunteer their time once a month. They don't see the same patients every visit. I don't have a doctor because we don't have any health insurance."

"Well it don't matter, you gonna be alright and the baby too."

"Yeah, now what's your goood news."

"Oh I almost forgot. It don't seen all that great no more. It could never top your news."

"What is it anyhow?"

"I saw a house. Now it's small and it needs lots of work

to it, but I figure me and Red can handle it. It's in North Charleston and I don't believe they can want too much for it in the condition it's in."

"Oh Nicky, that's great news. When can I see it? Did you take the sign down?"

"We can drive by there now. It won't look so bad to you in the dark. Get a pen and some paper to write the realtor's phone number down. You can call them in the morning."

Nicholas drove Natasha to the house. They got out of the truck and walked around the house. They tried to see through a window but it was too dark to make out anything inside. Still they were caught up in the moment and they agreed that this was their house. The next morning, Natasha called the realtor and made arrangements to pick up the house keys during her lunch hour. At twelve noon, Nina drove Natasha to the realtor's office, then on to the house. The condition of the house was really discouraging, but the hopes of owning her own home lifted Natasha through it. The house was eleven hundred square feet. A small house with five tiny rooms; two bedrooms, a kitchen, a living room, a dining room and a bathroom. The house had a small fenced-in back yard. The floors in the bathroom and kitchen needed to be replaced. The roof was old and needed to be repaired with new shingles. The wood on the front porch was rotten. There were a few broken windows and the whole place needed to be painted inside and out. Nicholas and Billy Joe will whip this place into shape she thought. Natasha imagined everything about the house as it might be, her heart beat with excitement, and she imagined she felt the baby move.

The house was so economical, the ten-percent down payment and closing costs only used up half of the money that Natasha had saved. They used the rest of her savings to buy materials to repair the house. Half way through the repairs, when Natasha's growing stomach was just beginning to show, they moved into the house. Billy Joe took the smaller of the bedrooms. Natasha explained to Billy Joe and to Nicholas that this arrangement was fine until the baby was a year old and ready for its own room. These days were filled with excitement, joy and merriment. Nicholas, Billy Joe, and some of their friends worked on the house every evening and all day on Saturdays and Sundays. Natasha got her work schedule arranged so she worked until three in the afternoon during the week and had the weekends off. Almost everyone they had ever known pitched in to help however they could. The women were helpful keeping things in order and preparing the food. Natasha floated on air. She fed everyone and made sure there was always plenty of beer in the coolers. The guys joked around as they worked. Every session was filled with gaiety and ended with marijuana and whiskey. When the house was all completed, Nicholas and Natasha gave a party that lasted an entire weekend. The house had been transformed to a clean, brightly painted and completely habitable dwelling. Natasha was openly prideful and for the first time, something gave Nicholas a degree of self-satisfaction. Nicholas always felt that Natasha was what motivated him, but now he came to realize that Natasha was guiding their lives towards success. At last, he came face to face with her ambition. The first night of the party, he resolved in his mind that he would do everything he could to encourage her leadership. He would clear the path before her and follow.

North Charleston is a fairly large and developing town with all kinds of stores and shops, selling a wide variety of goods, but Natasha could not find a maternity shop. She was half way through her pregnancy and showing. They had the house half furnished and now she felt it was time she bought some maternity clothes. Someone told Natasha about a store in downtown Charleston called "The Second Time Around." The shop sold recycled infant and maternity clothes. The place was on King Street bordering a black community. One morning Natasha had Nina drive her downtown to find the shop. They drove around until they found it, but there was no where nearby to park the car. They had passed a parking lot three blocks away, so Nina let Natasha out in front of the shop, which hadn't opened yet. She would drive back to the parking lot, have some breakfast at the corner coffee shop and walk back to the maternity shop. Natasha stood in front of the shop looking at the displays in the window when an old black man standing in the doorway of the adjoining shop called out to her. She looked around and pointed to herself in a "Me?" gesture.

"Yes, come here," the old man said. "They're not opened yet."

Natasha was hesitant at first, but she didn't feel threatened by the old man. She felt more curiosity than fear. The windows of the shop were crudely painted with the twelve signs of the zodiac. The bordering walls surrounding the windows were painted black with clumsy painted stars. On one side was a painted red ball and on the side an orange ball, representing the sun and the moon. Over the door in white paint was the words "Life Universal Knowledge." Natasha walked over to the old man. He was dark black. He had white hair and a short white beard and mustache. His face was kindly and the depths of his eyes were like the ocean. He was dressed neatly in a tattered brown suit, blue shirt and red tie. He grabbed her hand and led her into his shop. His hands, soft and pliable, felt like a balloon near full with warm water. The place had the sweet pungent aroma of burning incense. Flickering candles and the light that came in from the outside mixed to give the dim room a bizarre feel. The walls were lined with books. A cluster of folding chairs leaned against the far wall next to a lectern. The ceiling was painted blue with stars and planets peaking out like at the planetarium. There was a long wooden table surrounded with chairs, in the center of the room.

"I'm waiting on my friend to meet me at the store next door," Natasha said, as a precaution, although she still felt safe.

"We'll look out for her," the old man said as he gestured for Natasha to sit. "I want to take you to your future."

"You want to what?"

The old man got a burning candle from the bookshelf and placed it on the table near where they sat.

"You have a strong aura," he said. I felt your presence over quite some distance."

"You what?"

"Your magnetic field, the atmosphere around you emanates a signal that I feel. I call it your aura. Everybody's got it, but some are stronger than others. Yours is very strong."

"My what?"

"You have an old soul, from another time and another place. I recognize your soul like I know it. We are old souls together. What is your name child?"

"Natasha Hilgrown."

The old man wrote the name in the center of a full sheet of brown paper with a pencil. He balled the sheet of paper up and placed it in a metal bowl on the table. He lit the paper with a match. As the paper ball burned, its ends unfolded and swayed. The old man held Natasha's hand and paid strict attention to the movement of the slowly burning paper.

When the paper was all consumed, he closed his eyes and held Natasha's hand over the bowl.

"Look at my face he said softly."

Natasha was now curious and amused. The old man's face took on the look of pain and anguish.

"This child you carry will bring grief and self doubt at first. The child won't be normal and you're going to wish that you had done some things differently. This child will bring you anguish, pain and ridicule. Over time, this same child will bring joy, understanding and be the origin of great personal growth for you...and then there will be two more children." This said; the agony on his face was released. He rubbed a finger over Natasha's wedding ring.

" You will have a bigger ring and yet another bigger ring, but you will always be willing to give up all rings to keep the ring giver closer to you. Some of the old habits of the old generation will separate you over trying months time and again. " The old man chuckled. The old man's eye popped opened for a tenth of a second like a blink in reverse.

"Not one, but two college degrees will acquaint you with the fact that accomplishments come not solely from scholarship, but all the matrix of life applied." The old man had a look that suggested his pleasure at this articulation.

"You will achieve a sizable house with guarded and fastened doors that will end your lust for the comfortable feeling of status and instead you will long for the contentment of a home. And, you will have a pool and two dogs, but even they will not end your search. Such attainments will only provide temporary pleasure and the realization that they are barren of what it is you truly seek. It is only after you seek and obtain oneness with all your endeavors that serenity will become possible."

"I really gotta go. My friend is outside waiting for me," Natasha said pulling her hand away gently.

This guy just pissed her off, talking about her baby. She had thought about giving up drinking and smoking, cigarettes and marijuana. She had heard that they could have bad affects on the baby, but she didn't believe it.

The old man released Natasha's hand and opened his eyes. He was trying to re-focus his eyes, and bring his mind back to the present.

"There is more," he said.

Natasha didn't understand all that she had heard. She didn't know why, but most of what she heard made her feel uncomfortable, like walking on unstable ground. And, what she heard about her baby made her dizzy.

"No, I really gotta go," Natasha said rising from the table. The old man still sat at the table. She shook the old man's hand and returned to the street. Nina was in front of the maternity shop looking around for Natasha. When Natasha reached her, Nina handed her a container of hot tea.

"I though you might like this hot orange flavored tea. But before we go inside the shop, please tell me what in the hell were you doing in that place there?"

Natasha looked over to the painted windows, "Fumbling in the dark, in a search for the future," she said.

"Huh?" Nina asked.

"Searching, just searching."

AT THE SPEED OF LIGHT

Anecdotes never travel unmolested in Kingsville, a hamlet inhabited by colorful embellishers. To embellish is more than a town tradition; it's a distinctive feature of our people. I love my town and the people, and I wouldn't say anything to malign them. I've lived here and been amused by it all of my life. So, when I reveal this aspect of my town's peccadillo, I do so not to make mockery, but rather to display its honor. For fear of having my name attached to the handiwork of fanciful imaginations, I shouldn't tell it, but I also fear that not to tell my name would place my credibility in doubt. So, for the sake of credence, my name is Otis Pringle. I've owned and operated a barbershop on Church Street by the courthouse for forty years. I know the people here as hard working, patriotic, God fearing, and honest. We are a people anchored by a basic respect for honesty, which makes our inclination for embellishments a competitive and pleasurable recreational pursuit.

No one in Kingsville has ever caught a small to average size fish. Such a fish is the one caught by the fisherman down the riverbank. Every fish ever caught by a Kingsvillian has an uncommon attribute; the ability to grow in the accounts of how, when, and where they were caught. I recognize tales that originated in Kingsville from all others mostly by the scent. There is a certain relish to the enhancements of Kingsvillians that stands out plain as day to me. No two accounts of any one event ever to happen in Kingsville have ever been recounted in just the way it originally occurred.

When old lady Grace Hudson was startled by a small chicken snake in her flower bush, she later told Mr. Jake, her next door neighbor, about the four-foot snake. Mr. Jake told Buttermilk, the town's mechanic, about the six-foot snake. Buttermilk told Cadillac Brown, who owns one of the town's two national franchises, a Kentucky Fried Chicken operation, and the story traveled on. The story was retold a dozen more times. When it reached the ears of Valerie Hudson, Grace Hudson's sister-in-law, the snake was a ten-foot rattler that hissed, rattled, and scared poor Grace Hudson into bed. Valerie and old lady Hudson married two brothers who are both now departed. Grace Hudson and Valerie Hudson are as affectionately attached as blood sisters. Valerie was so upset at the news that she cooked up a pot of shrimp gumbo right off and took it to her sister-in-law to cheer her up.

Grace Hudson is seventy-five years old. Her hair is long and silver gray. She is a tall slender woman, erect and as healthy as the American economy during the Clinton Administration. Twelve years earlier, Ben Hudson, her husband, was killed in an automobile accident the very morning he retired from the Highway Department. Her two daughters are married, and live out of state with their own families. Grace Hudson's great joys are when her daughters and their families come to visit in the summers and her many flower gardens.

While Valerie served up the shrimp gumbo, garlic bread, and sweet tea on the front veranda, she recounted yet another enhanced version of the snake event, and expressed her concern for Grace Hudson's safety. The two ladies sat in the shade two mighty oak trees pitched onto the veranda. The scent of shrimp gumbo mixed with the fragrance of the flowers that surrounded the veranda created an aroma that delighted the two ladies. Grace Hudson is extremely fond of Valerie's shrimp gumbo. Valerie Hudson goes to great lengths to prepare the dish. Every ingredient has to be absolutely fresh. Her okra is pan fried before it is added to the pot. Her tomatoes are vine ripened and picked only minutes before they are needed. The shrimp are few, but large and only added to the pot after the fire under the pot had been cut off. To Grace Hudson's thinking, Valerie's attention to these details makes all the difference. Grace took a tiny taste of gumbo and contemplated Valerie's stated concern, but she couldn't mount an effort to correct Valerie's version of the snake event. "My dear," she did say, "this gumbo is divine. Lord knows how you do it"

Once, a small fire caught up in Alex Thompson's kitchen while he was rushing fish to fry on too high a flame before the start of the football game on television. The fire was easily put out before it did any real damage. Still, by the time the story of the kitchen fire reached the other side of town, it had almost burned Thompson's house down. Alex Thompson has had to cook for himself for the last three weeks because his wife left him to live with their son and his family in Atlanta, Georgia. Alex Thompson had been a domineering husband with a gruff manner. He wears a thick mustache and he is far too much over weight. After twenty-five years of trying to please him, Mrs. Thompson momentarily gave up, although, in her heart she still loved him. Her move, she knows, and he knows, is temporary, and a last resort to get his attention concentrated on her discontentment. Although, Thompson is a hard working man and a good provider, his real loves are fried mullet fish, beer and football. Over the years, Mrs. Thompson's existence in his life had become incidental when compared to these things that brought Thompson his sense of gratification. And, unless Mrs.

Thompson doesn't quickly negotiate some concessions with her husband that will allow her to return with enhanced dignity, Alex Thompson may yet burn his house down.

Junior Mercer is a young man of chance. He frequents the few notorious spots that exist in town. Junior is a happy go lucky, good-looking boy who, three years ago, right before he turned twenty, achieved his one ambition, to finish high school. Junior is a charming rogue and he drives a fine automobile. Parents of the town's young ladies go to great lengths to keep their daughters distracted from him. He works odd jobs now and then, but through good luck and cunning, he keeps money in his pocket. Junior Mercer once broke a two-day card game in the back of Wally's Quickstop. He walked away with all of one hundred and ninety-six dollars and fifty cents. The next day Junior received requests from several of his buddies, each wanting to borrow a few hundred dollars of Junior's winnings. Junior's buddies, you see, had talked with losers at the card game, each claiming to have lost several hundred dollars.

Such is life in the town of Kingsville. These enhancements are able to prosper because they travel from person to person or among small groups. Many times, I have wondered how these distortions would straighten themselves out if they were all assembled at one time in one place in the presence of their inventors. Would the aberration of the many versions of events overload the town's perception of reality and give the town a nervous breakdown? Would the townspeople repudiate the embellishments and live in one truth? Or, would the clash of the embellishments create chaos and hostility? The answers to these questions were soon to come.

These are the facts of life in the town of Kingsville. And, who better to tell it? I can say that I am the only person in this town without a penchant to send the facts traveling out to yonder. I will submit, here and now, however, that in all other ways, I am a Kingsvillian. There are three barbershops in town. Mine is the busiest and the only one open five days a week. I've got three chairs and during the holidays and the start of the school year, my shop is so crowded, I rent two chairs out to other barbers. Everything that goes on in Kingsville is critiqued in my shop. I hear several versions of the same event in a matter of hours.

Kingsville is a small hamlet west of the Ashley River. We are a crab, shrimp, and mullet eating people. Our population is near nine hundred, no one knows for sure. The Census people have never accurately counted us, but I'm willing to bet that the county Tax Assessor's office knows our numbers. We are a prosperous tax paying community. When you drive through Kingsville on Highway Seventeen, the plaque at the town-line reads: **YOU ARE NOW ENTERING KINGSVILLE, A SMALL TOWN WITH A BIG FUTURE.** There isn't a sign to tell you when you're out of Kingsville.

Johnny Gibson is the town's mayor. He is a tall athletically built forty-two year old man, with a youthful appearance. He played football in high school and in college and he looks today like he could still run a touchdown. He married Loretta Wilson, a bright and pretty girl he met at college. He brought her back here to start their lives together. They have two teenagers, a girl seventeen and a boy thirteen. Back then, when Johnny graduated from college, it wasn't yet profitable for employers to appear equitable, so they didn't hire college educated blacks in any managerial positions in this area. The textile plant had just opened up and was hiring laborers. Johnny got a job at the plant and today he is a shift manager.

Johnny Gibson is an attractive, easy-to-like politician. Ever since Johnny was a teenager, he's had these little gray patches of hair over his temples. He has always got a smile and a kind word for everyone he meets. He is only the second mayor we've had since the town became incorporated, and he is as popular amongst Kingsvillians as rightwing political dogma is at Conservative Concerned Citizens meetings. It was the people in Johnny's church who first noticed his leadership gifts and suggested that he run for mayor. Now, let me tell you, we're a small town, but we're big on churches. There are fifteen different churches of all sizes and affiliations. If you're in town on a Sunday, there is a church here for you.

Anyway, Johnny ran for mayor and won. Since he's been mayor, he's brought in a sewage waste system and got the town wired for cable television. He's been a good mayor and done the town proud. So good in fact, we just recently re-elected him. After the mayor was re-elected, he promised to give a victory party for the entire town regardless of how you voted. He wanted everybody in town to be present all at one time, something that had never before occurred. The mayor's re-election celebration was going to be the first time every living soul in Kingsville, and by extension, every distortion ever told in Kingsville would be at one place at the same time. The big test for the town's sense of reality would arrive on that day.

In preparation for the party, Johnny took a day off from work to go catch some crabs. He is an excellent crabber, as is everyone in Kingsville. He has caught crabs at the same spot in the creek ever since he was a boy. Kingsvillians know the crabs in our section of the creek and the crabs know us. There is a constant mutuality between us—also with the fish and the shrimp. We catch crabs with chicken backs and necks these days. When I was a boy, in a less prosperous time, people went bogging bare feet into the creek with a forked stick and a sack. Back in those days, if your household had chicken backs and necks, there was no immediate need to go crabbing. There isn't a man, woman, or child who, after filling a cooler or bucket, doesn't leave whatever chicken is unused for the crabs to eat. It's a part of our need for reciprocity with the creatures of the creek.

The mayor had six pieces of strings tied to chicken backs in the water on one end, and to a marker stick pushed down in the mud bank of the creek on the other end. He moved from string to string pulling them in close enough to net up the crabs eating on the chicken backs. In two hours, the mayor had filled one cooler and half filled another. He had more crabs than he could haul back to his pickup truck in one trip. But the urge seized him to fill the other cooler, partly because he wanted enough crabs to host a crab crack to thank the town's people for re-electing him. And partly because...well, you've got the idea, Johnny Gibson is a Kingsvillian. Johnny continued to catch crabs oblivious to his surroundings. He never noticed when a three-foot alligator swam thirty feet to the right of where he stood and eyed him hungrily. After a moment, the mayor got the feeling that he was being watched. He looked up and was startled by the sight of the alligator in the water so near him. He took a hurried step backwards and bumped into the full cooler of crabs. The mayor was now concerned enough to appraise his catch in a more realistic light. He threw the rest of his chicken backs into the water to give thanks for his catch and hauled the coolers, one at a time, back to his truck.

We Kingsvillians believe this generosity enchants the creatures of the creek and perpetuates the crab's taste for chicken. There is a story of a Kingsvillian who caught five bushels of crabs and didn't leave a thing for the survivors. This Kingsvillian took his unused chicken back home with him for his next outing. Well, legend has it that that person never caught another crab from this section of the creek, ever again.

Later that evening, after all the regular business at the Town Council meeting had been discussed, the mayor told the four members of the council about the alligator in the creek. He told his story just as it had happened, except the three-foot gator had grown to five-foot, and the mayor had three coolers not two. This upped the stakes so close to the date of the big test. The mayor, unconsciously had begun another embellished story that would grow and gallop through town like a delirious horse, and could, like all the others, adversely confront the townspeople when they assembled for the celebration.

Alabama Brown, is a member of the Town Council, the brother of Cadillac Brown, and the owner of the other national franchise, a Burger King which sits across the road from the Kentucky Fried Chicken place. Alabama Brown ran against Johnny Gibson in the last election and lost, but kept his council seat. In all the years, Brown had been a member of the council, he never once discussed accounts of the councils meetings with his wife, but the mayor's folly was another matter.

This is the version of the mayor's encounter with the alligator, Alabama Brown told to his wife during dinner. "The mayor went to catch crabs on the very same day that a seminar on government grants to small municipalities was broadcast on ETV. The mayor could have used this time to learn how to apply for federal dollars to build the gymnasium we need," Brown said, although he didn't watch the program himself.

"The mayor spent the entire day trying to catch a few dozen crabs," Councilman Brown told his wife. "It got late and the tide was rising, when the mayor, frustrated by the crabs' cageyness, walked out into waist high water. Not even a man that desperate can catch crabs this way." Brown said looking into his wife's eyes. "The mayor should buy groceries sometimes and stop trying to feed his family from the creek,"

Brown grumbled, between spoonfuls of shrimp gumbo and rice. "I have never known a man so cheap he would risk his life trying to sneak a few crabs from a new born alligator lost from its mother. There ought to be a law against this kind of thing," Councilman Brown said in mock anger. "This is the kind of thing that goes on in a town that doesn't have the insight to elect the right man mayor. It ain't good that Johnny Gibson is mayor of Kingsville," Brown concluded. Councilman Brown's wife, an educated and ambitious woman who wanted her husband to be mayor—for her own grandeur, retold the story in yet another fashion, to people who authored even other details.

Mack Gibson is the mayor's cousin and a member of the Town Council. He is the mayor's most ardent supporter on the council. Mack Gibson is thirty-eight years old and he resembles the mayor in looks and statue. He also works at the textile plant and is a supervisor in the division that produces carpet backing. Mack Gibson is married and has a ten-year-old son. He is exceedingly proud of his cousin and would follow him to hell and back. He wants his son to be just like Johnny Gibson.

"The mayor," Mack told his son, in his account of the story, "wants to give a crab crack for the town to celebrate his victory. Your uncle gave up a day's salary to go to the creek by his lonesome to catch enough crabs to feed the town's people at the victory party. There just isn't another person in all of Kingsville who cares for the people like Johnny Gibson. There isn't another person in town who would wrestle one alligator to feed the town's people, let alone three. I love the people of this town and I hope to be its mayor's someday," Mack Gibson admitted, "but even I don't have that kind of gumption. It was nothing short of a miracle that cousin Johnny was able to win his foot back from the clutches of that alligator's jaw with all the other ones trying to take a bite out of him. Johnny Gibson brings pride to the Gibson name and to our community. One day he will be the governor," the father predicts to the son. Mack Gibson Jr. listened to the story intensely. He knew that his father had told him something of significance. When he retold the story, he out done his father in detail and drama, but still not the drama his listeners would later add.

Deacon Oscar Jones, the third member of the council to hear the mayor's story, is a carpenter by trade. He is also a member of the Board of Deacons of the Righteous Road Church of God and Christ. Deacon Jones is sixty-nine years old, and the oldest member of the council. He has always been a man of reason and compromise. Whenever the council was deadlocked on an issue, Deacon Jones prayed for guidance, which always seemed to come moments after one of his thunderous and lengthy prayers. Deacon Oscar Jones has lived a long life directed by his belief in Divine signs. Deacon Jones navigated the unknown by his interpretation of the signs God laid in his path.

Deacon Jones told the mayor's story at a meeting of the Board of Deacons with the zeal of a Baptist preacher. "The devil finds work wherever he can," Deacon Jones began, "in high places and low. Mayor Gibson's name was on the devil's work sheet. How it got there, God only knows. What we all know is that Mayor Gibson is a good man. A God-fearing man, but he was overtaken with the sin of greed and there is a price to pay for every sin. My brothers, we have all got to recognize where the limits are and draw the line right there- if not before. Brothers, we have all got to live every aspect of our lives guided by His hands. Johnny Gibson fell prey to greed— the devil recognized what he saw and turned himself into an alligator to test the mayor's faith. Why, that's the devil's job here on earth—to test our faith. The devils' been working at his specialty, which is temptation, since the time of Adam and Eve, and he's gotten pretty good at it. And, if you ask me the devil wins, more victories then he deserves.

"There's not a man at this table," Deacon Jones continued, "who don't know the greatness of God. Our God is ever vigilant. He watches over vagabonds and viscounts, sinners and the saved. Ours is a triumphant God. What else could have brought our mayor back from the teeth of the devil, but the touch of God's goodness, grace and mercy? Johnny Gibson is a blessed man who God has placed among us for yet unknown purposes—ain't God great, ain't God's mysteries sweet? Ain't God's mercy divine?" Deacon Jones had them nodding in agreement and shouting "Amen, amen, amen brother."

There were nine members of the Deacon Board who heard Deacon Jones' sermon. These are all hard working, rock solid, devoutly religious men, and members of the largest and most respected church in town. When God delivers a sign to these men, they feel compelled to reveal *it* and reveal *it* in all *its* magnified glory.

Councilman Ned Ford owns and operates a place called the Crab Shack. They sell barbecue ribs, grilled chicken, boiled crabs, fried fish, and steamed oysters, from Thursday to Saturday night. The Crab Shack is located on a side street in an undesirable section of town and it's a popular place although its surroundings are old and unkempt. It is mostly our underprivileged citizen's who hang out there—but the food is clean and tasty. It is widely believed that bootleg whiskey is sold there after Red Dot hours, but there have never been any disturbances, so they are left alone.

Ned Ford is Councilman's Brown's political ally and they

are both members of the Kingsville Business Association. It was before a gathering of the town's businessmen and women that Ned Ford offered his account of the mayor's alligator incident. Ned Ford's voice is high pitched and crackles nervously. "I sell crabs," Councilman Ford said at one point during his tirade, "live and cooked. I buy my crabs from professional deep-sea fishermen. My crabs come from deep uncontaminated waters and are safe for people to eat. For years now I've been telling town folks that the waters where they crab are contaminated with chemicals from the aluminum plant up the river. Most people believe I say this to protect my business and they continue to eat crabs from dirty waters. Well, I can't stop that. This is a matter that we've dealt with in Town Council meetings so the mayor is fully aware of the condition of the creek. The mayor wrote a letter to the manager of the aluminum plant complaining about the pollution. So, he knows the condition of the crabs from that creek. I don't know why the mayor didn't come to me and I would have donated some crabs for his celebration, but no, he would rather serve people polluted crabs." At this point, Councilman Brown cleared his throat rather loudly. Ned Ford got the message. "The election is over. It's time to bring this town together. We all have to celebrate the town's decision, so I'm gonna donated to the mayor's victory celebration anyhow. Councilman Brown and I have teamed up to donate two bushels of crabs, five bushels of oysters, and a tub of fish." Then Ned Ford smilingly said, "There will be other elections."

This meeting of the Kingsville Business Association ended in anticipation of the victory celebration, which was the next day. Over the next hours, the story of the mayor's alligator incident traveled from person to person at the speed of light. It spread out over the town like the tentacles of an octopus with versions from the near factual to the outer reaches of the absurd.

The victory party was held in Robert Smalls Park, two blocks from Town Hall. The trees in the park were all decorated with colorful balloons and ribbons. A local five-piece band played popular tunes and old blues standards from a small platform that was erected for the occasion. All businesses were closed for the day, and all of Kingsville was on holiday in the park. There was a festive mood in the air. Tables were set up throughout the park and staffed by members of the churches, the business community, the volunteer fire department, and the town's police department with all kinds of foods, sodas, and cakes. The children played about the park. Some children climbed trees trying to haul down balloons; others stood in food lines. Some of the older children played a loud game of volleyball. Grace and Valerie Hudson sat on a bench at the entrance to the park. Half the town's folks paraded through this entrance. Most of them stopped to offer greetings and make small talk about the fine weather and the jovial mood before they moved deeper into the heart of the festivities.

The mayor's official table held the crabs he caught, cooked and ready to serve. A mound of steamed shrimp, and a mound of potato salad, also garnished the table. Johnny Gibson, his wife, and their son and daughter stood to the side handing out paper plates and chatting with the people around their table. The mayor's family beamed with pride as people patted the mayor on the back and made complimentary comments on the fine job he was doing as mayor. And, while Kingsville's finest and most respected citizens clustered around the mayor's table, the largest and most festive crowd was at the table shared by Councilmen Brown and Ford. Their table was set up across from the statue of Denmark Vessey, a block away from the mayor's table. A large tub of crabs steamed in beer sat on the ground next to the table. Lemon wedges and crab seasoning gave the tub of crabs a mouth-watering appeal. There were pans of fried fresh mullet fish that covered half of the table. Ned Ford fried the fish himself on the spot, in a deep fryer behind the table. On the other side of the table were plates of glittering oysters on the half shell. Two shapely young women with saucy smiles and tight jeans opened the oysters and kept the plates full. A loud and boisterous crowd hovered around this table continuously. They were all in a frisky and playful mood, but if there was any whiskey drinking, they kept it well out of sight. Junior Mercer stood in the center of a group of rambunctious young men who flirted with the two young women opening the oysters. They babbled about the sound of the audio systems in their cars, whether Michael Jordan was the greatest player ever in basketball, and the latest hip-hop jams.

The band stopped playing and Reverend Lewis Michael of Mount Zion Church walked to the microphone on the platform to start the ceremony. He led the gathering in a recital of The Lord's Prayer, after which, he introduced Sarah Wright, a gifted young girl who sang the National Anthem. Then he introduced Louis Osgood, who is near ninety years old. Louis sang the Negro National Anthem in an old crackling voice that would have pleased James Weldon Johnson. Then, Reverend Michael introduced the mayor with a volley of sentimental words.

The mayor gave just the right speech for the occasion. "I'm not going to take up much time from the festivities," he began. "I simply want to thank everybody for the confidence you've placed in me. I want you all to know that I appreciate it, and I won't let you down. Now I want everyone to have a good time and let's see to it that the young ones have a good time. There's plenty to eat and lots of sweet tea and sodas, right here in the greatest little town in all the world." As the mayor stepped away, the band started up with a rendition of "Ain't No Stopping Us Now."

Deacon Oscar Jones sat at a table near the platform with the Reverend Michael and a group of churchmen from all the different churches in town. The conversation was high-toned and religiously pitched. The men each took turns interpreting this or that quotation from the bible. Alex Thompson roamed the area of the park where Ned Ford fried fish. He munched on fried mullet sandwiches with mustard and ketchup, making sure not to get too far from Ned Ford's deep fryer, and telling anyone who would listen that Mrs. Thompson had called and that she was returning that very next day.

The day ended as it began, in harmony and with pride. There was not a word spoken about the snake in Grace Hudson's flower garden. No one broached the fire in Alex Thompson's kitchen. Junior Mercer's winnings from gambling went unmentioned. Nor, was the mayor's alligator incident discussed. Not one version of these or any of the other thousands of exaggerations that float around town from time to time was mentioned while the entire town was assembled as one on this day. I came to understand that this is achieved through an intuitive social agreement to avoid awkwardness. Not a conscious, spoken plan, but an extrasensory miracle. It seemed there was a telepathic arrangement that danced unseen from Kingsvillian to Kingsvillian to prevent the collision of perversion. I also came to understand that there wasn't any need for this social contract to be premeditated because all kingsvillians subscribe to the theory that there are no falsehoods, only distorted truths. In Kingsville, everything, to some degree, is true.

CAPTAIN'S CREEK

Rufus Bates was returning home on his bicycle from the general store in Ridgeville, where he bought two cans of sardines and a small loaf of bread for supper. The bread and sardines swung from side to side under the handle bar in a brown cloth sack, as Rufus peddled down Highway 27. Rufus Bates was an old man. His health, while not the best, was pretty good for a man seventy-five years old. On this score, he had no complaints. For years now, however, his hearing had been failing him.

"Rufus Bates."

Rufus heard his name called out and looked around but he didn't see anyone. He peddled on, thinking, perhaps, he had said his name in his mind.

"Rufus Bates, pure soul," he heard again.

Rufus stopped peddling and dismounted his bicycle to look around. He was on the overpass covering Captain's Creek where people usually fished. One favorite spot is on the banks under the overpass. No one fished there now. Rufus looked all around. He looked into the thick trees that lined the highway and saw no one.

"Over here," the voice cried out.

The old man gently laid his bike down on the shoulder of the road. He took a step towards the railing then remembered his supper sack. Sack in hand, Rufus walked over to the railing on the overpass. There he could see the creek below. This was where the sound seemed to be coming from. Still Rufus saw no one.

Rufus Bates lived alone and since his retirement from the sawmill ten years earlier; he had very little contact with other people. He talked with town folks on his monthly visit to the Post Office to get his social security check. He didn't mind mingling on his short, but frequent trips to the general store. His closest neighbor lived a half-mile away; a distance that grew longer with time. Rufus had lived alone for so long he grew serene and comfortable with his solitude. He spent many of his evenings in long periods of silence. During the months of good weather, he would sit near the window and clear his mind as the sun disappeared over the trees. By dark, he would be in a trance. Rufus also talked to himself. He developed the habit of talking to himself some years after his young bride died. He talked to himself in the house when he cooked or cleaned and while he worked in his garden. And, he sometimes heard voices. But the voices Rufus heard never clearly uttered words; they were hums and chants. This voice he now heard called his name and although he heard the voice several times now, Rufus wasn't sure that it was real. Rufus walked his lanky body over to the end of the railing and climbed down the embankment to the creek bed. The tide was low and narrowed the stream. Rufus looked far down the edge of the creek to a familiar tree and a spot where there used to be a clearing.

"Over here, pure soul," the voice groaned.

Rufus quickly turned his head in the direction the sound came from, but all he saw was a fish. The fish lay on the bank just a few inches from the narrowed stream—a fish inches out of the water. Rufus examined the fish carefully with his eyes and thought the fish was dead it lain so still. The fish was a foot long with silver skin glaring through its scales. Rufus thought the fish looked like some kind of bass, but, then it had a look all it's own. He walked closer to get a good look at the fish. As Rufus bent over the fish it wiggled ferociously, flinging itself a few inches into the air then falling back down to the bank.

"Thank you for hearing me."

These words seemed to come from the fish. The old man bounced upright so quickly he almost flipped over backwards. He looked to the sky through the trees and put his hands to his ears, his supper sack slapping the right side of his neck. After an instant, he bent over the fish again feeling it was best he quickly disbelieve what had just occurred. The fish had a hook with a few inches of broken line in its upper lip. The fish was still now. For this brief moment it was possible for Rufus to believe that he merely misunderstood what had happened. He was after all, an old man, and reality sometimes lies, even to old men. This thought was comforting until words came from the fish again.

"You're pure enough of soul that you can hear me, but you can't recognize me from my appearance when I saw you kiss the girl on the creek bank."

The fish wiggled less fiercely this time; just enough to change its position on the bank.

" I can use your help. If I don't get this hook removed and return to the creek I'll surely perish."

"Help you?" Rufus answered more as a reaction to the voice than to the fish. Rufus wondered how the fish knew his name. But if this fish talks what difference does it make that it knows my name, Rufus reasoned. The old man felt he was engulfed in a dream where what happens happens. He had no intentions to talk back to a fish. Had he been conscious he would have said nothing. Had he been awake none of this would be happening. "Help you how?" The old man repeated.

"The hook, good hearted man. The hook must be removed."

The fish wiggled more vigorously than the last time, but barely lifting itself from the mud bank.

"Dear pure soul, if you would remove this hook, you could then throw me back into the creek and be on your way."

Still in what seemed to be a dream, Rufus picked the fish up and tried to take the hook from its mouth. He pushed in and up on the hook, but the hook tore deeper into the fish's mouth. The pain sent the fish wiggling from his hands back to the creek bank. Dream or reality, Rufus sensed he needed to act deliberately. He picked the fish up again and put it into the sack with the bread and the sardines. He rushed back up to the road and mounted his bicycle. Rufus peddled as fast as he could. He passed people working in their yards who hailed him and wished him a good evening. He saw them all and may have even heard them—he acknowledged none. The fish was the only thing in his consciousness at this moment.

Rufus arrived at his small three room wooden house out of breath. He took the cloth sack from the handle bar and threw his bicycle to the ground in one motion. He pushed through the unlocked door of the house. Rufus placed the sack on the kitchen table. He hurried over to a drawer in the corner of the kitchen where he kept some hand tools. He searched frantically, throwing tools to the floor, as the fish wiggled the sack open. Finally Rufus found the wire cutters. He ran back to the table and picked the fish up from the sack. He held the fish tightly under the gills until its mouth opened and the hook could be seen clearly. The outer edge of the hook was rusted, but the core of the metal was firm and strong. Rufus cut the hook in several places, letting the pieces fall to the table. He lay the fish on the table next to the sack with the bread and the sardines. Rufus sat in a chair with his elbows on the table and his hands to his cheeks. He looked at the fish shaking his head in disbelief and amazement.

It had been a while since the fish moved and it hadn't spoken since they left the creek. Rufus took stock of the fish's condition. It breathed heavily; its gills opened and closed in distress. Water. Water, Rufus thought. He went to the sink and ran some water into a drinking jar. Rufus gulped the water down and ran out the door with the jar still in his hand. He ran to the back of the house and rinsed out a tin wash tub. He filled it near full with water but he couldn't lift it. He poured the water out until the tub was light enough for him to carry. He hurried it into the house, but the water level was now too shallow. Rufus filled a basin from the sink and after many trips to and from the sink, he had the tub nearly full. The fish was on the floor wiggling desperately, swallowing eagerly for water. Rufus picked the fish up and eased it into the tub. The fish laid on its side and floated motionlessly on top of the water. Then the fish wiggled like a limp whip. Then it wiggled and wiggled in jerking motions. Then it swam frenzied to the bottom of the tub and back up and around and around, like a dazed prizefighter trying to clear his head. Finally it splashed water from the tub, then settled down realizing the tub's perimeter.

Rufus sat at the table to eat his supper of sardines and bread. He dropped some crumbs of bread into the tub and watched mesmerized by the fish. Rufus relaxed his body. He dispelled all thought as he hummed a full round sound that resonated in his vibrating body until his mind was empty and the sound filled the house and lifted it into the heavens.

For most of the night, Rufus was in a dream state. He dosed and he was near consciousness. He dreamt about his young wife who died after giving birth to their premature child. The dream started with the day Rufus first became aware of Birdie in the churchyard after an Easter Sunday service. Her real name was Alfredia Gillard, but everyone called her Birdie. She wore a white dress that matched the whiteness of her teeth. Her black hair glistened and was plaited into two ponytails. Two white bows hung on the plaits. She was a tall dark skinned girl with a big smile that made everyone take notice. Birdie was seven and Rufus was nine. They and the other children of the church ran about the yard laughing excitedly. They were hunting Easter eggs, pulling and pushing each other and having great fun. Each time Rufus found an egg; he grabbed Birdies' hand and pulled her to it. Then he ran off in search of the next egg. At the end of the hunt, Birdie's basket had more eggs then any of the other children. Rufus kept one egg for himself. This was the day that cemented their friendship and their all too brief future together.

Rufus and Birdie saw each other at the church three days a week. They both grew up in poor, but devoutly religious families. They were in church almost all day every Sunday. Wednesday nights were devoted to prayer meetings. Choir practices were held on Fridays. Rufus and Birdie spent as much time together as possible during the days and evenings at the church. But they didn't see much of each other at the one room schoolhouse. As he grew up, Rufus didn't attend school on a regular basis because he worked in the fields to help his sharecropper family.

It first became clear to Rufus that he would someday marry Birdie at a Sunday church picnic at a cleared section of Captain's Creek. The entire congregation gathered dressed in their very best clothes at this cleared spot of the creek, which flows from the Edisto River. Birdie was now fourteen and

Rufus was sixteen. After a fire and brimstone sermon from Pastor Sanders, and a meal of fried chicken, greens, yams, rice, watermelon, cake and churned ice cream, Rufus and Birdie went off to explore along the creek bank. They walked hand in hand occasionally throwing pebbles into the water. When they were far enough from the others, they ducked behind a tree and kissed for the very first time. It was a short innocent sweet kiss that sealed the fate of the two.

"Y'all ought not ta do tha. Y'all ought not ta do tha in front da fish. Y'all ought not ta do tha in front da fish fo ya done fright dem off." A high pitched voice called out, startling the young lovers.

They looked down and saw that the voice was that of an old man, who sat fishing, his back leaned up against the very next tree. He wore rags. His hair was long and matted. A white beard covered most of his black face. His eyes were red as the sun and something white oozed from them. Green snot hung from his nose. His teeth were uneven and brown. It was a man neither Rufus nor Birdie had ever seen before, but each had heard talk of. This man was known as "Old Slavery" because he was born during the time of the great tyranny. He lived in a shack down the creek, and, it was said, he talked out of his head and fished all the time, but no one ever saw him catch a fish. All kinds of ghostly and mythical notions had been attributed to this mysterious figure in the woods. It was even said that he wasn't human at all, but a spirit lost in time, with the ability to appear in different forms. The unexpected voice startled Rufus and Birdie, but the sight of the man terrified them even more. They slowly backed away from the man swallowed up by fear. Then that fear turned them around and they ran as if for their lives.

"Cum ta scare way ma fish ya da cum fo scare way ma

fish." The high-pitched voice crackled in the air and followed them back to the clearing.

Rufus dreamt about his months of work trying to finish their house before the marriage. Although the house wasn't completely finished by the wedding day, it was livable. Rufus and Birdie were married at the little Holiness church where they worshiped all their lives. It was a sun bright Saturday. His white suit and her white dress glared during the ceremony. Their families and almost all of the forty-member church attended. After the wedding meal, they were driven to Summerville to have two wedding pictures taken. One picture of them together and another picture of Birdie alone. That night when they were to themselves the moon shone bright as a barn fire in the distance. This was the happiest night of their lives. Music from the radio flowed throughout the window of their unfinished palace. Rufus and Birdie, exhilarated by the events of the day, danced playfully under the moonlight. Cripple Clarence Lofton sang "Strut That Thing" while they frolicked until the early morning under a happy sky. By the time they had fallen asleep, Bukka White sang "Fixin' to die Blues" and the moonlight dimmed towards the West.

Birdie was pregnant by their first wedding anniversary. Rufus was beside himself. He worked hard all day at the sawmill and at night in his garden. He looked forward to becoming a father and these thoughts heightened his happiness. But for Birdie, it was a difficult pregnancy. She felt sick all the time. In the fifth month she was stricken and had to take to her bed. Each day Birdie drank an herb blend the local midwife sent to her that did little good. She was young and strong so no one thought that it would end as it did. One morning early in Birdie's seventh month of pregnancy, Rufus had to get the midwife. Birdie screamed with pain until evening when the baby finally arrived. It was a tiny boy child and it came into the world dead. It was the worst day ever, despairingly bitter, a day that gave voice to all the blues songs ever sung. The next morning Birdie was still in shock. She spoke to no one. On the second morning, before Rufus went to work, she told him how sorry she was. When Rufus came back from work, Birdie, swallowed up by grief, lamented her deep sorrow. Before Rufus went to sleep that night, she told him how sorry she was. The third morning, she said nothing. Birdie, suffering from a profound sadness, a broken heart, and the lack of antibiotics, had joined her unnamed boy child in death. Rufus died a death of his own; a death of the spirit from which he would never recover. Rufus had intended to name his son so God would know how to call his earthly spirit, he just never got to it.

Rufus was born into a church, which taught that the innocent suffers for the sins of the world. Rufus wore his burden like a badge of honor. He would suffer, but he would never share the melancholy of his burden with another. He was never to remarry. He worked at the sawmill and over time saw less and less of his relatives and neighbors. In the first years after the death of his wife and child, Rufus went often to the graves in the small cemetery at the Holiness church. It was when the church closed and Rufus became cut off from the church community that he became reclusive. For over half a century, Rufus lived the life of a hermit and now all he had were two aged photographs and his ancient memories.

The morning sun beamed through the window onto the table awakening Rufus from a sound sleep that followed hours of a mystic dream state. He spent the whole night asleep in the chair with his head on the table. Rufus awakened conscious of the fish's presence and a new recognition. He stood up and stretched, then he sat back down and looked at the fish in the tub. The fish, its tail fin barely moving, hovered in the same spot slightly submerged in the water. "Good morning," Rufus said to the fish, not knowing what to expect. The fish swam to the bottom of the tub, hitting its nose against the side as if it was trying to swim through it. Rufus got up from the table and heated water for tea. He washed his face and rubbed his few teeth with the wash rag. After a jar of hot tea and a slice of bread, Rufus used the basin to take two thirds of the water from the tub, and then he replaced it with fresh water. Rufus looked at the fish wondering what should become of it. What should he do with it? "Don't you have voice this morning?" Rufus asked. "You only have voice when you need help? You kin talk in the creek, but not here huh? "

Rufus kneeled over the tub. Using both hands, he grabbed the fish up from the tub and put it in the cloth sack. He hurried out the door and mounted his bicycle. He headed for the cemetery where Birdie and his unnamed son were buried, the fish swinging in the sack under the handle bar. The cemetery ground was overgrown with grass and weeds. Although it had been years since he had been there, Rufus went directly to the graves. There was one simply inscribed stone to mark both graves. Alfredia Bates and Son, 1921/1940. Rufus stood by the graves for a short while, then knelt down and put his hands to the ground. "Your name Alfred," he said. "God been calling you by your eternal name, cause I never named you. God needs to know your earthly name for this life. Your name Alfred Herman Bates. Now God know to call you what I call you. Then Rufus remounted his bicycle, feeling light-hearted, invigorated, and peddled hurriedly to Captain's Creek.

Rufus walked to the spot where he first kissed Birdie and

the tree where they saw Old Slavery. He kneeled over the creek bank and held the sack over the water. Rufus jerked the sack upwards letting the fish fall to the water. The splash made a perfect circle that widened rapidly as the fish swam free and quickly disappeared into the deep of the darkened water. Rufus followed the spiral of the water with his eyes until he reached its finest point. He felt for a moment that he no longer stood on the bank of the creek, but that he was in the eye of the spiral, where right below the surface, redemption resided. He walked over to that familiar old tree. Rufus sat down. He leaned his back up against the tree. He pulled his knees towards his chest and wrapped his arms around his knees. Then Rufus slowly hummed his mantra: Ummmmm. Ummmmm. Ummmmm.

A FAMILY GOES TO AFRICA

When his sister Beverly told him that Akbar and Marvia had become engaged, Reginald knew instantly that he would fulfill his dream of seeing some part of Africa before his sixty-second birthday. When the telephone conversation with Beverly ended, Reginald sat silently savoring his on-the-spot decision to be at the December wedding in Cape Town, South Africa. Akbar was Beverly's son and Reginald's nephew and although Africa was a long way to go for a wedding, he felt obligated to be there in support of his family. He wanted Marvia's family in South Africa to see this generation of the Morrison family of America, as it had always been; united, supportive, and now, middle class. Reginald saw himself as the patriarch of the family and he wanted to wave his family's colors. Then, as with all things too sweet to digest, reality arrived on the scene. Emily, Reginald's wife, is a financial fretter who opposed his proposals intuitively. He knew that she would raise the question of the cost of flying from Charleston, South Carolina to Cape Town, South Africa. He was confident that the idea of going to Africa would be so overwhelmingly appealing to Emily that she would soften any objections that she might have against making the trip.

Reginald carefully thought out a plan to broach the subject to Emily. When she got home from work, he cheerfully made his presentation. He explained that he would search the Internet for the cheapest tickets available. It was March and the wedding was nine months away, so they had time to purchase the tickets far in advance to further ensure a decent price. Reginald suggested that other family members would probably go along. He beamed at how unique an experience it would be, to have a sizable segment of the Morrison family in Africa for the wedding. As Reginald expected, Emily did raise the question of cost, but only in an apathetic manner; after all, she saw it as her duty to slow Reginald's spending, so she made an automatic, meaningless mention of cost. Emily's attraction to the idea was immediate and obvious. During dinner, they shared a stimulating conversation about Akbar and Marvia's wedding and about how wonderful it felt to be going to Africa.

Two years earlier, Akbar had gone to the University of Cape Town as an exchange student. It was there that Akbar met Marvia and they became friends. Over the weeks, Marvia took it upon herself to show Akbar around Cape Town and the surrounding areas. A romance began to blossom between the dark skinned boy from New York City and the colored girl from Cape Town. In a short time, Marvia took Akbar, whom she talked about all the time, home to meet her family. Alfred and Lisa Moore had an older married daughter, Virginia and a 21-year-old son David, who still lived at home. The Moore family embraced Akbar and demonstrated their acceptance of him from the very beginning. When Akbar returned to the United States, he and Marvia kept in touch by telephone. The next year Marvia got an exchange student position at the University of Sarasota in Florida. The program provided a month of travel at the end of her stay. Akbar drove his twelve year old maroon Mercury, a gift his mother had given him when he entered college, to pick up Marvia from Sarasota and drive back to New York City. On the drive back, they stopped at the homes of Morrison family members in Florida, South and North Carolina, Maryland and Pennsylvania for a few days stay at each home.

This is how Reginald and Emily got to meet Marvia Moore, the light skinned, articulate and pretty girl who referred to herself in the racial classification term of apartheid South Africa. Reginald cringed to hear Marvia say the term *colored*, but he and Emily fell instantly in love with her and did their best to make the short visit pleasant and memorable. Reginald took the lovers to catch crabs one morning. That evening when they were all out in the yard enjoying the crabs and beers, Reginald and Emily saw that Akbar and Marvia interacted with the ease of two people who had already bonded for life. Their interplay radiated the sense that they were deeply in love and would soon marry. On the day they left for the next Morrison household, Emily and Reginald agreed that marriage was in the air. At the end of their journey, Marvia spent a few days in New York and Pennsylvania before she returned home. Akbar graduated from college that May and, as he had planned, joined the army. He was just completing his training in the field that would be his military occupation when the surprised September 11th attacks on America took place. The attack in New York City, brought down two buildings Akbar grew up viewing from the windows of his family's Bronx apartment 15 miles away. Akbar and Marvia made plans to meet after Akbar finished his training, but after the attacks it became impossible for Marvia to get back into the United States, so they agreed to meet in London for Christmas. They spent the holiday week in London and this time together consolidated their devotion to each other. At the beginning of 2002, Akbar received an assignment in Germany and in March, he was able to return to Cape Town. This is where Akbar proposed marriage and Marvia accepted. Time made true, Emily and Reginald's prediction and now here they were, making plans to attend the wedding.

Reginald sat outside on the kitchen steps to smoke a cigarette as he telephoned his brother Randy in Walnut Creek, California. Reginald broke the news to Randy, but he didn't have to ask Randy if he was going. Randy immediately said that he would start searching for tickets for himself, his wife Naomi, and their daughter Nikki. Randy was sure that their son Hugh, a reporter in Atlanta, would not find the time to take off, but he would approach him with the idea anyway. Reginald and Randy discussed whether their mother who was 79 and sickly would want to go. They thought that she would pass on this trip because of its length, and, in any case, Ruth, their sister, who looked after their mother, would oppose. They laughingly agreed that Ruth wouldn't go. No one has ever been able to get Ruth on an airplane. Some year's back, Ruth made a three-day journey by train from New York City to visit with Randy and his family in California. Beverly could count on her sister Ruth, to be supportive, but she would not board an airplane, so Africa was not in the plan for her. Reginald declared that none of his three married sons would be able to make the trip for a myriad of reasons. Beverly, her second husband Ronald and her grown daughter Katherine would form the nucleus of the wedding party of eight. At this point, it was unclear if Andrew Cornwall, Beverly's first husband and Akbar and Katherine's father would join the group. This said, Randy and Reginald made plans to keep each other informed on what each found out about airline ticket prices.

During the next several weeks, the wedding party heated up the Internet exchanging dozens of emails daily. Marvia searched about in Cape Town for lodging for the group, while everyone else concentrated on the ticket search. By the end of May, everyone had purchased tickets. Marvia starting making everyone familiar with Cape Town by emailing links to popular sites in and around the city. She made sure everyone understood that it would be mid-summer in December when they arrived. "You will be coming from the cool to the heat," she said. The search for affordable housing went on. Marvia sent some prices for renting a house that brought everyone's attention to the exchange rate between the dollar and the rand. In early June, the rate was $1.00 to 10.03 rands. This turned the 8000 rands for rental of a four-bedroom home, Randy and Reginald considered, into an affordable 800 dollars for ten days. Randy and Reginald sent a deposit for the house. Beverly and her family booked rooms at one of Cape Town's four Holiday Inns, and everyone settled in for the passage of time.

In late August, Reginald received an email from Beverly saying that Akbar would be getting in touch with him. Reginald and Akbar were closely attached. When Beverly and Andrew separated and then divorced, Reginald and Emily still lived in New York City, so Reginald started spending more time with his sister's two children, but particularly with Akbar. The children were very young and Reginald wanted to make sure that they had a male role model in their lives. So, when Beverly emailed that Akbar would be getting in touch with him, Reginald immediately thought that this was to ask him to play some role in the wedding. Reginald couldn't imagine what that might be, but his chest swelled with pride, as he waited to hear from his nephew. Days went by without Reginald hearing from Akbar, then on the last evening in August the phone rang. It was Akbar on the line, "Uncle Reginald," he began, "there's good news and there's bad news. Let me start with the bad news. The wedding is off."

The shock was so sudden Reginald nearly dropped the receiver. He didn't know what to say. Reginald had been married to Emily for 38 years and some of her tendency towards ominous thinking had rubbed off on him. So early on in the process, the thought had once, just briefly, crossed his mind—what if the wedding was called off after we had paid for our tickets and put a deposit on the house? Reginald dismissed the notion; he had seen the love between Akbar and Marvia, pure and as unassailable as the Pope's dignity. He was certain that this would never happen and the possibility never entered Reginald's mind again. "What happened?" He asked. Then without giving Akbar time to answer, he said, "Who called the wedding off?"

"Uncle Reginald I don't want you to be angry with her, but Marvia called the wedding off."

Akbar's tone and his plea for compassion awakened an acute awareness in Reginald. He needed to stay in the moment and be in full command of all his faculties. He needed to be open and understanding, as well as encouraging and sympathetic. He took some deep breaths to sharpen his perceptiveness.

"I know you've spent a lot of money to come to the wedding..."

"Akbar, don't worry about the money," Reginald interrupted. "That's not important at the moment. We love you and we love Marvia. Do you understand that?"

"Yes, I love you too, Uncle Reginald."

"Good, now tell me what happened."

"Uncle Reginald, Marvia and I have some religious differences that we can't seem to work out. She's a Christian and I told her that I respect that. I don't understand why she can't respect what it is I believe."

"You mean she's broken off the wedding because you practice Buddhism?"

"Exactly."

"I don't understand Akbar, Marvia is a bright young lady, I wouldn't think that she would let something as benign as Buddhism hinder the happiness you two are headed towards."

"I know," Akbar said. " We had other issues also and we went to counseling and worked out everything but this. I even told her that she could raise our children as Christians and that I would go to church. I mean, what else can I do?"

"What you did was right. You see how benevolent one who is on the path to enlightenment can be?" Reginald said. "Does she still love you?"

"Uncle Reginald, I'm sure she does. She says she does and I know she does. And, I love her very much."

"Akbar," Reginald said, "this sounds to me like a bout of marriage jitters. Everything will work out. Don't worry, she'll come around. I know that the love that you two have for each other is stronger than anything—even this misconception."

"I just wanted to talk with you because I felt bad about you spending all that money. Anyway, if you still decide to come, Marvia and I will show you a great time. I've been to some good jazz clubs in Cape Town; you'll love it. You will be able to increase your African art collection. There are open-air markets all over the city. When they see that you're an American—even a black American, they are all over you for that dollar."

"Akbar don't worry about us. We're coming. Look, have Marvia give me a call."

"I will Uncle Reginald, but please don't be angry with her."

When Emily got home from work, Reginald didn't say

anything about the phone call. He thought it odd that Akbar said that he and Marvia would show the wedding party a good time, when it now appeared that there would be no wedding. This was also a hopeful sign. Akbar had not cancelled his month-long leave of absence from his unit in Germany, so he was holding on to something. The next morning Reginald called Randy to bring him up to date on the state of affairs. At first Randy was dumbfounded, then he exploded with anger for buying the tickets so early. Reginald told Randy that he had decided to go ahead with the trip and that he thought things between Akbar and Marvia would be reconciled by then. Randy decided that he would have Naomi look into what they could do to return their tickets. Randy speculated that they might get vouchers to fly to some other part of Africa at another time. Reginald found it difficult to make Randy understand the obscurity of the problem; he hardly had a grasp on it himself. Reginald told Randy that he was expecting a phone call from Marvia and that he would let him know how that worked out. He asked Randy to keep him informed on the ticket situation and said goodbye.

The next day Marvia called. The fact that she called confirmed Reginald's suspicion that this might be a temporary situation. If she really intend to drop the wedding, why would she consult with her fiancé's old Uncle from South Carolina? After some congenial greetings, they got right to the question. There was anguish in Marvia's voice, which changed her speaking pattern and thickened her accent.

"Akbar said you wanted to speak with me," She said.

"Yes, I want to try to get an understanding of the problem that made you call the wedding off," Reginald said in a friendly tone." Now I hope that you won't consider this meddling, but I hope that I can get an understanding that will help me to say something that will be useful."

"No. Not at all, Uncle Reginald."

"I've heard Akbar's version. Now I'd like to hear how you see things—what the problem is to your mind."

"Uncle Reginald, Akbar and I have come a long way. We've gone through so much together in a short space of time and he has matured a lot since we met."

"I understand from Akbar that the problem is religious in nature."

"I don't what to dominate Akbar. He says that our children can be Christians and that he would go to church, but I worry that I'm asking too much of him. I just don't know what to do. I don't want him to make all the sacrifices for our marriage"

"Do you love him?"

"I do. I really do."

"Then isn't that what really matters."

"I don't know. I really don't know, Uncle Reginald.

"Look Marvia, I'm an old man, I've been around for a while and I've experienced a lot in life. I know that these things have a way of working themselves out. You're concerned about Akbar's acceptance of Zen Buddhism, but I think that you can see that all that has done for him is to concentrate his mind and give him focus. I'm kind of a Zen Baptist myself, so I know that his reading on Buddhism is harmless to him, his behavior and your relationship."

"We've still trying to work things out. We talk every day on the phone."

"Look, I think that what you're going through is really very normal. You just need to clear your mind and give the issue a chance to surface clearly. I think everything will work out, but I want you to understand that I'm not trying to convince you in one way or the other."

"Thank you, Uncle Reginald."

It was during this part of the conversation that they lost connection. Marvia made the call on a pre-paid phone card and the time ran out. Reginald felt heartened by the tone and content of the conversation. That evening he finally told Emily about the situation and the conversations. He explained to her that he was confident that the wedding would happen as planned. His take was that Marvia was just a little nervous. He told her that Randy was looking into returning his tickets. He said that he would look into it also, but he was sure that the tickets were non-refundable. I think the wedding will happen, he concluded. But when he talked with other family members, he joked that he was going to issue an edict preventing the Morrison youth from having relationships with Africans. Reginald would mention a Morrison niece who had eloped with an African man whom he had warned against because the man was a Nigerian. The man was found out to be a swindler and the marriage failed in short time. Now here was another African who was disappointing another Morrison youth. An edict banding all such relationships was definitely in order Reginald would joke. "No more Africans."

Beverly hadn't called or emailed Reginald since the call telling him that Akbar would be getting in contact with him. In fact, for this period, all communication between the wedding party lost momentum and excitement. When Beverly did call her brother, her tone was aggrieved and apologetic. She wanted to know what he planned to do with his tickets. Reginald quickly assured her that even if the wedding was off, the trip was still on if only to fulfill his long time dream of visiting Africa. For over thirty years, Reginald made vague plans for going to the slave states of West Africa, where most black Americans came from, and in the last five years he had even set up a savings account just for that purpose. It was a cause that pulled him in the way Jews gravitate towards Israel. So, the trip was on, but Reginald felt in his gut that the wedding would still take place. Reginald waited a few days before he spoke with Randy again. Randy's wife found that it was impossible to return their tickets and they had now decided to make the best of the situation. The wedding being called off had marred how they all felt about the trip somewhat, but the momentousness of making a trip to Africa, in a family group, was nothing to sneer at.

In mid-October, Reginald returned from the mailbox looking over the mail. Among the bills and advertising flyers was a brown envelope with neatly hand-printed letters addressed to Mr. and Mrs. Reginald Morrison. Aside from the neatness of the printed letters, the envelope didn't garner any special attention from Reginald. He opened it when he got to it in turn. It contained a wedding invitation, printed directions on a card and a store gift registry card. Reginald looked at the envelope; it had a South African postal stamp on it. He opened the invitation and read:

Together with their families
Marvia Moore and Akbar Cornwall
Request the honor of your presence
At their marriage
Thursday, the 12th of December
At 17:30
Langverwagt Farm
Please RSVP by Nov. 30th.

Reginald called Emily at work and excitedly told her about the invitation. His excitement emanated more from the fact that he felt vindicated for believing the wedding would go on than from receiving the invitation—he kept the faith. Reginald called his sister Beverly and his brother Randy to share in the joy. Then he called other family members who weren't going to the wedding, but were expecting to send gifts. Everyone he called had received an invitation from South Africa. None of them had ever received mail from abroad before now and they were all delighted to be included in this mailing.

On December 9th, Reginald and Emily were among the last group of the wedding party to arrive in Cape Town, along with Beverly, Ronald and Katherine. Randy, Naomi and Nikki had arrived the day before. Andrew, the father of the groom and Beverly's ex- husband bought a ticket during the last week and was the first among the wedding party to arrive. Akbar had arrived from Germany ahead of everyone. He and Marvia took a taxi-van to the airport each time someone arrived to haul them to their lodgings. After the last group arrived and had freshened up, they all met at the home of Lisa and Alfred Moore. The Moore's are of Indian and Malaysian ancestry and are classified as colored in the South African racial designation system. They were exhilarated to have the Morrison family, whose hues ranged from black as Akbar to light skinned as his mother Beverly, in their home and soon, permanently in their lives. Bubbling with excitement, the Moores showered their guest with graceful hospitality. Lisa was so excited she made offer after offer: water, fruit, juice, wine and cheese, music, television. Then she explained that reservations had been made for dinner at the Blue Dolphin Jazz Club for that evening, but there was still time for a visit to downtown Cape Town and she offered to be the group's tour guide.

Akbar had arranged for two taxi-vans to be always available to the wedding party. All they had to do was call and a taxi would meet them where they wanted. The drivers were instructed not to accept any money, Akbar would take care of the cost after the wedding party had gone back to America. Lisa called for one of the taxis and in a short time they were downtown, looking every bit the tourists and attracting lots of attention from the local inhabitants. Lisa explained that this was just a preliminary trip to get a feel of the city. There would be time on other days to visit the museums, the Wharf malls and many other sites. The wedding party resembled a group of small town visitors in mid-town Manhattan. That evening at the Blue Dolphin Jazz Club, they were all in an exhilarated mood. The waiters had put four tables together and arranged an eye appealing setting before they arrived. There were the nine members of the wedding party, Alfred, Lisa, their son Hugh, their daughter and son-in-law. Marvia and Akbar sat next to each other glowing with pride and joy. Their eyes sparkled with anticipation. After everyone ordered dinner and the wineglasses were filled, Alfred made a toast, and then everyone stood up one by one to make a gleeful affirmation on the joy each felt. Akbar was the last to speak and he finished his speech by asking Reginald to act as master of ceremony at the wedding. Reginald emotionally agreed as everyone cheered. As the evening wore on, members of the two families mingled from group to group, laughing and getting acquainted.

The next day the wedding party split up; some went on a tour of the wildlife areas, some to the museums, some to the casinos. They had agreed that they would go together on the emotional trip to Robbens Island, where Nelson Mandela and the leadership of the African National Congress had been imprisoned. And, that they would all share the thrill of the cable ride up Table Mountain. That evening Alfred took everyone to a Reconciliation Concert at the outdoor stadium. Reconciliation Day is a national holiday in South Africa and there are activities all over the country in celebration of the country's racial détente. At the concert in Cape Town, there were many bands, dancers, speeches and the Talking Drums. Midway through the evening five drummers mounted the stage and begin to pound the drums. At one point during the drumming, everyone in the stadium started to laugh and as the drummers played the laughter became even more robust. Everyone in the wedding party from America was stunned. Reginald, who sat next to Alfred, asked what happened. "Oh, I'm sorry," Alfred replied. "The drums told a joke. I can't translate it, but it is a very funny joke about apartheid." Reginald wondered what could have been funny about apartheid, and then he remembered the long list of Jim-Crow jokes blacks in America told each other as a part of their survival mechanism.

The wedding was to be the next day at 5:00 p.m. Reginald had gone to one rehearsal to learn his role as master of ceremony. The wedding would be held at the Langverwagt Farm, an old family winery in Zevenwacht village 35 miles from Cape Town. The setting was stunningly suited for weddings. The flower garden and a fountain were to one side of the main building that had a tavern, banquet hall and dance floor. The main garden had space for more than a hundred chairs and a flower canopy. As master of ceremony, it would be Reginald's responsibility to get people moved from one section to the next, to welcome everyone as a group once they were seated in the banquet room, to make a short introduction and to announce the speakers. That morning Reginald sat at the desk in his room and he wrote:

Welcome, welcome, welcome.

My name is Reginald Morrison. I am the oldest Uncle of the groom.

Today it is my most pleasant duty to bid you all greetings on behalf of the Moore Family and the Morrison/Cornwall family—on this very special occasion—the joining together of two families from two distant parts of the world.

This is a momentous achievement in itself —but not nearly as consequential as the fact that two young people have offered each other their eternal love before us all and under God.

THE HISTORY OF LATERAL # 7

I came by my penchant for candy in an innocent manner. One might even say it was the result of my early ambition and industry. When I was 10 years old, I obtained a position at Al and Ben's Candy Shop. My daily duties included mopping up after closing, maintaining the comic book racks, stocking up the soda cooler and the candy cabinet. I arrived at 5:00am on Sunday mornings to collate the separate sections of seven different newspapers before the rush of people returned from sunrise Mass. I stayed to sell candy to the kids returning from morning Mass at St Paul's Church.

Al and Ben's Candy Shop was the name of the establishment although its main trade came from over the counter, where sandwiches, hamburgers, cakes, pastries, milk shakes, egg creams, cigarettes and newspapers were sold. This was the heart of the business, but it didn't escape my attention that the emphasis in the store's name centered on a glass cabinet against the wall near the rear of the shop, which I commanded. The glass counter had six shelves that held candy and bubble gum. It had sliding glass doors that I slid open to serve pointing customers. "Please don't touch the door," was my regular refrain to eager candy buyers on Sunday mornings when I reigned supreme. The year was 1951. I had no idea that this would be the beginning of a 50-year saga with lateral number 7.

Albert Loeb and Benjamin Stein were Jewish merchants

from the Bronx. They were partners in the candy shop on Amsterdam Avenue in mid-town Manhattan. Al was a jovial man for whom life was an amusement park and baseball was its main feature. Al admired Jackie Robinson, not because of Robinson's stunning athletic abilities, but rather, because Robinson broke the color barrier in baseball and made it possible for Willie Mays to play for the New York Giants. Al Loeb loved The New York Giants and he loved the "Say-Hey-kid." During the baseball season Al was continually lauding one or another of Willie May's breath-taking breadbasket catches. Al excitedly described how Mays turned his back to the ball hit high in the air, then caught it running towards the outfield wall. Al also spent considerable time cursing the jinks that kept the Giants from winning the majority of the subway series with the Yankees and the misfortune that kept them from becoming World Series champions since 1933. Al was the partner who hired me to the position of candy stock-boy. In 1954, the poltergeist of baseball rewarded Al with a Giants' World Series for his congeniality with a little black kid from the projects.

Ben Stein was an unhappy man. He always called me Rote instead of Rudy. My full name is Rudy Brown, but Ben sometimes called me Rotten Town. It seemed a dark cloud hovered about his existence. Ben was always grumbling. He drank gallons of carbonated water to settle his stomach and he didn't care for baseball. On Sunday mornings when the coffee had brewed and we paused in our work to have breakfast; Ben always served me stale pastry. It was Ben who limited my salary to five dollars a week. There was no divine reward for Ben, just dark clouds. Perhaps liking baseball makes for a better personality.

It was while I worked at Al and Ben's Candy Shop that I

began eating more candy than was healthy for lateral number 7. Because I complained that my pay was not commensurate with the many skillful services I performed, Al attached a few fringe benefits to keep me happy. At the end of the month when the comic books that hadn't sold were to be returned, I got to keep a few. Each night that Al closed the shop, I could bring home a pocketful of candy for myself and my younger brother and sisters. There were times when I stood in the back stockroom and unseen gobbled a candy bar down.

Squirrel Nuts were my favorite candy and I should have learned a valuable lesson from an experience that I had eating them before I began my career as a candy stock-boy. It happened in the schoolyard during recess. I was in the third grade. One day I returned to the schoolyard from the candy store with a nickel's worth of Squirrel Nuts. My baby lateral number 7 had been loose for a week. The first piece of Squirrel Nut candy I chewed on wrapped around the tooth and held to it with such strength that the tooth gave way and came out in the candy. I learned nothing from that experience and continued to eat as much candy as I could buy.

When I landed my plum position with Al and Ben, my supply route to candy increased enormously as did my proclivity to eat the stuff. The stock room was in the rear of the store. Back there were shelves filled with boxes of: Oh Henry, Baby Ruth, Butterfingers, Squirrel Nuts, Mary Janes, Mars Bars, Jelly beans, Jaw Breakers, Mounds, Almond Joy and chocolate bars. My proximity to this part of my work strengthened my love for it. My affinity for candy lasted past the period when the demolition teams tore down the houses and stores on Amsterdam Avenue and the construction crews built Lincoln Center for the Performing Arts on the site where the candy shop once stood. This displacement had a great impact on me. This was my introduction to the impermanence of things, until then I thought that all that was would always be. By then my permanent lateral number 7 was in place. A high brow Arts center replaced the candy shop. Now I no longer had access to free candy so it cost me a small fortune to ruin the new tooth as, in time, was done.

When I was 15 years old, I notice a brown spot on the lower edge of lateral number 7. I didn't go to a dentist because there was no pain. In the fifties, dentist offices were viewed as chambers of torture. Most people I knew went to the dentist only when they were tormented with pain. Besides, I lived in a poor family; there was no money for repairing a tooth that was poorly treated in the first place. That summer, I met a girl named Catharine Russell and fell immediately in love. She was 15 also and she was very mature. She was a light skin girl with reddish hair, bright eyes and an attractive face. Her figure was still developing, but I could tell that she would one day be comely. Catharine was unlike the other girls in the neighborhood because she could talk to boys without being all girly; her femininity appeared to be induced by her very nature. She had full lips that were sculptured beautifully, but when she opened her mouth to talk or laugh, she exposed a mouth full of cavities. Catharine's teeth were pitted and hollowed with brown rings around each cavity. Here was someone who had done to many of her teeth what I had only begun to do to lateral number 7. I was so captivated by Catharine that I told myself that even her cavities were cute and I continued to admire her. Finally, late in the summer of 1956, she noticed my affectionate fascination for her and rewarded it by accompanying me to a movie theater on 42nd Street where we kissed in the dark and I fell out of love.

I joined the army in February of 1960. I went through an

extensive physical examination, but if I saw a dentist, he must have disregarded the worsening condition of lateral number 7. It had a small hole at the bottom, which I was fond of sticking my tongue in to feel the sharp edges where the candy had eaten away the tooth. After completing all of my basic training and the airborne course, I was assigned to a unit of the 82nd Airborne Division at Fort Bragg, North Carolina. Now I was allowed to keep some personal items in my locker. I was 19 years old and still had my affection for candy, so; of course, my locker remained stocked up with many kinds of candy. Whenever we went on field exercises, I supplemented my rations with candy.

I took candy everywhere, even to Washington D.C., in January of 1961, when my unit went to march in the inauguration of President John F. Kennedy. We were housed at an Air Force base in Virginia. The first night there we were allowed to go to the enlisted men's club to drink beer. I had just recently taken to drinking beer and my affections for it would, at times, rival my affections for candy. Paratroopers are tough and they are always eager to demonstrate their stamina. After a few beers, a fight broke out between a group of paratroopers and some flyboys at a near-by table. In short order, the fight spread from table to table. Soon everybody in the club was fighting. The flyboys were badly outnumbered and had to retreat from their own club. No one was badly hurt, but the next morning our commander had us running in formation around the base shouting out apologies in cadence. We weren't given any more free time until after we marched in the inauguration. Inauguration day was so cold that a Milky Way could freeze without being refrigerated as I had done habitually. That night they let us loose on the town. The next morning we loaded into our buses and headed back to Fort Bragg.

I was in Fort Bragg during the tense period of the Bay of Pigs Crisis. One night when my unit was on high alert, they roused us out of the sack and we dressed quickly. We were issued our weapons with live ammunition and then they trucked us to the Pope Air force base, where the C-130's were ready. We were airborne for a while, but I can't say where we were headed, then after a while we landed back at Pope. You can bet I had candy bars with me that night. As history would have it, that war was averted, but the crisis caused me to further damage lateral number 7. A year later, I went through another world crisis with Kennedy. I was transferred to Bamberg, Germany in early 1961. In Europe, many new kinds of candies were exposed to me. I loved the sweet almond chocolates from Switzerland and the German thin chocolate wafers. I was becoming an international candy connoisseur. I was intoxicated with the discovery of so many new forms of sugar to put lateral number 7 to work on—and, visa-versa. Months after I arrived, the Soviet Union and the East Germans erected the wall that divided East Berlin from West Berlin. In the first months after the wall went up, the newspapers were fill with pictures of people trying desperately to escape from East Berlin. Many of these people were shot to death. Some were captured and the lucky ones made it to the West. Once again, I was in a unit that was issued live ammunition to save the world from tyranny. These were nervous months for me that required lots of soothing candy. President Kennedy came to West Berlin and declared "Ich bin ein Berliner," and again, war was averted. The wall didn't come down for another thirty years. I was discharged from the army in 1963. Kennedy moved on to focus on Vietnam, and his re-election campaign. By then, an eighth of lateral number 7 had rotted away. When I looked in the mirror at the tooth, it reminded me of Catharine Russell, although, unlike Catharine, I had one tooth ruined. I was now 21 years old and had seldom ever been to the dentist.

November 22, 1963, was another cold day. I had a job with a company that made attachments for sewing machines for the garment industry The union I was a member of picked the busy holiday season to strike the garment industry's shops. That Friday I walked the picket line outside the company where I worked. An old neighborhood friend walked by accompanied by a young lady. They stopped to tell me the news that President Kennedy had been shot and that my friend was getting married that night. My friend introduced me to the young lady with him; they worked at the same company. She was going with him to the flower shop to help him select flowers for his bride and the wedding hall. My friend had not invited the young lady to his wedding, but because we were old friends, he asked that I come to the reception. I asked the young lady if she would accompany me. As it turned out, President Kennedy died that day; I escorted the young lady to the wedding reception later that evening. Eight months later, I married her.

1968 was mostly a dreadful year. The war in Vietnam was raging. The year began with the assassination of Martin Luther King. The middle of the year brought the assassination of Robert F. Kennedy. 1968 ended with the vicious Democratic National Convention and police rioting against political protesters in the streets of Chicago, and I started working for the New York City Transit Authority. I got a good paying job with real benefits. I had job security, health insurance, vacation time, sick pay, a fifty-percent pension and dental insurance. My life was enriched by the many benefits my employer provided—all but one.

In the summer of 1973, I was forced to the dentist with a bad toothache. The tooth was in the lower rear of my mouth and had to be extracted. Bad as lateral number 7 appeared, it was never painful. I never complained to a dentist about lateral number 7, and, up until this point, none ever offered any advice or course of action on it. After the extraction, I returned home, had some soup and lay on the bed to watch some television. There I saw to my amazement, the President of the United States of America, waving to his staff from a helicopter. The man, who in 1968, campaigned for the job by saying he had a secret plan to end the war in Vietnam, had resigned the presidency. His resignation didn't come about because his secret plan to end the war didn't work- although it didn't- but, rather, because his secret plan to get re-elected did work...for a while. I didn't start to use my dental insurance plan except, for emergencies, until a few years before my retirement.

In 1985, four years before I would retire, I started visiting a neighborhood dentist, not because of the quality of his service, but rather, because he was so conveniently located. I was 43 years old and the sight of half-eaten up lateral number 7 was now, finally, distressing. Although I started going to this dentist for work on another dental problem, he suggested that we also do something about lateral number 7. He explained the process and I agreed. I made several visits for a root canal and to get the tooth grind to a shaft and for fittings, that ultimately ended with a new lateral number 7. No, this was not the end of the saga with lateral number 7. It went swell for a while. I almost missed that brown spotted hole in my tooth. It took months for me to break the habit of rubbing my tongue up against the tooth in search of the cavity that was no more. Several years later while gnawing on some hot wings, the face of the tooth hit on just that spot that loosened it from the crown. The dentist was able to glue it back in place, but once the original factory bond was broken, the problem persisted. Each time the face came loose, I ran to the dentist to have it glued back in place.

I retired in 1989 along with Ronald Reagan and Ed Koch. My wife and I relocated to South Carolina. Now when the face came loose, I'd find the nearest dentist to glue it back into place. And, so it went, until in 1997, the face came loose and was lost. I went to a dentist who discovered that I needed major gum surgery to save not only lateral number 7, but also all of my other teeth. He referred me to a specialist, made up a temporary facing and plans to replace the whole thing using *new technology,* he convincingly explained to me. He would disassemble the whole thing, grind the shaft of old lateral number 7 down to below the gum, insert a pin into the bone, then cement a one piece crown onto the pin. The surgery and this process took a year to complete. When it was finished, I had healthy gums and a new lateral number 7 so perfect that my dentist took pictures of it and carried the pictures to dental conventions to challenge fellow dentists to identify the fake tooth from my natural ones. Whenever I went back to my dentist, he would brag about the tooth's great success stumping his colleagues. He was proud of his work on that tooth. I was also, but I wasn't hopeful that it would last. It didn't.

2000 came without producing the computer meltdown so many feared, and swept a second George Bush into the White House. Early in the year while I chewed on some hot wings, lateral number 7 broke off from the pin into two pieces. I was disappointed and depressed. I returned to the dentist. We started the process all over again. The entire pin that held the last lateral number 7 in place was not recovered from my gums, so a new pin had to be placed in a more awkward position in relation to the new tooth. Even my dentist didn't expect this tooth to last. He had none of the enthusiasm that the last tooth produced. He cautioned that the next step would be the more expensive tooth implant. I tried to avoid the expense of a tooth implant by being selective in what I ate and eating very gingerly. I was forever conscious that I had a delicate tooth in my month.

A month before the shrimp season of 2001, two airplanes with crews and passengers, had been hijacked by terrorist and flown into the Twin Towers in New York City where my saga with Lateral number 7 began. A third was flown into the pentagon. The fourth hijacked plane was averted from its target by the bravest of Americans. In October, my cousin invited me to shrimp with him on several different occasions. To fill an average size cooler with shrimps requires 3 to 4 hundred casts of the shrimp net. Each throw, the net is held between the teeth and has to be released precisely as the net is thrown. Bad timing results in an unsatisfying cast and loose teeth. I found casting for shrimp a stimulating activity, but I didn't think of what holding the net between my teeth was doing to lateral number 7. Pretty soon, I sensed a little play in the tooth—it had loosened. I returned to the dentist who confirmed my suspicion. Now I was at the end of the road with lateral number 7. My options were few, a bridge which would involve damaging other teeth. I decided to have the expensive implant done. This was a lengthy process of pulling the root of old lateral number 7, healing for a few months, then implanting the rod that would hold a new tooth, then healing for another few months. Then, at last, the new tooth, and it's a beauty too. It cost me a small fortune to ruin lateral number 7 and now it has cost me a small fortune to restore it. I've given up hot wings, casting the shrimp net and I haven't had a candy bar in...well, lets just say some time.

THE CULPRIT

I have a face that is known around the world, but I'm most infamous in the United States of America. It is there that I was born unknown years ago and it is there that I am propagated and nurtured. I am as much a symbol of American culture as baseball, but my appearances aren't seasonal. I am ordained whenever the need arises. A young white mother in South Carolina drowned her two sons by rolling her car into a lake. In her attempt to absolve herself of any blame in the crime, she lied that a black man had car-jacked her children. She gave a police sketch artist a description of me and for days, in front of television cameras, she tearfully pleaded that I return her children. That sketch appeared in newspapers and television newscasts around the world. I was once again boldly resurrected.

One day, a powerful white New York politician parked his car on the Manhattan side of the East River with a panoramic view of the industrial section of the Borough of Queens. Then this important official shot himself in an attempt to divert public attention from his corruption, and, perhaps, from the despair disclosure would bring. It was I whom he fingered from his hospital bed. I shot him, he said, in an attempt to rob him. He bravely resisted he lied. The picture of his empty car parked at the spot of the shooting was shown on television for a week with an appeal for information that would lead to the arrest of a shadowy black man fitting my description.

An unfaithful young white husband in Boston, drove his wife he no longer wanted, who was pregnant with a baby boy, he had not desired, atop an unkempt bridge in a black neighborhood and shot them dead. He knew that this was a prime location from which to launch his fabrication. He also knew what description to give in order to set the Boston police department on the lookout for me. The hunt began, as it has for hundreds of years, with compelling zeal.

That I am a convenient and believable scapegoat for white people with sinister motives, due to no fault of my own, is at the heart of my story, and is also a symptom of an incessant American illness. I tell my story in the protest style of the old Negro writers of the Negro Renaissance because so many people now proclaim that the time for that kind of protest has long past. I disagree—how can the time for protest have past when the reasons for protest has not? White people still find it easy to believe that I did it, whatever the it may be, because they know human nature. For half of the time I've been with them on this continent, they have denied my humanity, but now they accept and fear the reality that my instincts are, indeed, human ones. And, knowing human nature as they do, they reasoned that if my instincts are human, I would want to kill them for all they have suffered upon me. They know that this is how they would react had the shoe been on the other foot and in this sense, they inadvertently allow that I am the same as they. Whenever the alarm goes out for my arrest, they suspect that I am striking back at them, as they would do, for the centuries of harm they have heaped on me.

Then this murky distinction between that part of me that is the unreal—figment—of their minds and real black Americans exist. They confuse us for each other—they mix and match us whenever it's to their convenience. That I am not real sometimes escapes even me and I find myself referring to the real black people as me. It's a handy sociological tool that bridges the distinction between reality and expectancy.

This is exactly my problem. White people's expectation that I would retaliate for what they have done to me, allows them to believe that I would kidnap children, shoot a powerful politician, kill a pregnant woman, rape a hotel clerk, molest young boys, or even worse—I might want to share equally in the abundance of American life. It is the fact that they subconsciously anticipate a day when I will raise up to make amends that keeps my portrait at the ready in their minds. They have a collective expectation and a single image of me in their individual minds. Why else would a white woman in an elevator with a rich and famous black man fear for her pocketbook? She has perfect vision, but it is not with her eyes that she observes this man. She views him through the filter of her guilt and her fear. She knows that he should make an attempt to even the score and she sees this as his opportunity. The fear blinds her, she thinks he's me—the culprit—that one black man all white people carry around in their heads.

Now it's only fair that I point out that when I say all whites I don't literally mean all whites—but only that amount which gives the statement accuracy. This means that there are some whom I've malign—you know who you are—I beg your pardon.

Here is how I am most often described. I have a long face with full lips, a broad nose, sinister cheek lines and menacing eyes. I am brown skinned. I am sometimes drawn wearing the knit hat that was popularized in cartoon depictions of second story men wearing black masks, carrying a long flashlight and a sack of loot. I resemble no other black man in America, yet every black man in America can be mistaken for me, and many have fallen to that misfortune. It takes very little effort for those who describe me to verbally transmit my facial likeness to those whose fingers produce my image, because I am a exact figment of both of their imaginations—I am a figment of the imagination of every white person in America. Whether I'm tall or maybe just a midget is not known. It isn't even known if I have all of my limbs. Menace that I am I may have four arms and thorns for fingers. And, as allusive as I've been, I might have wings that enable me to swiftly perform my geographical gymnastics. I find it humbling that I have never been given a proper name, a situation that sometimes make it hard for me to grasp the reality of my existence. For the sake of this narration, let's anyone call me Leroy—no, make that Leroy the Culprit. Even that doesn't sit just right, how about Leroy the Phantom Culprit. Yes, now that has a certain ring of truth to it. Aha, you say, now you know who I am.

I'm not really a person; I'm a tool. It used to be that many white policemen in big northern cities, learned to carry an extra pistol or a knife with them. If they were ever involved in an unjustified shooting death of a black person, that extra pistol or knife became evidence to exonerate the policeman and justify the killing. I condemn the North for this practice, but in many areas of the country, this wasn't even a necessary nuisance. These are the tools white policemen used to protect and guide their careers in law enforcement. I am the tool white people utilize as subterfuge for the horrors they commit. Personally, I don't mind it for myself, but it does cause a lot of disruption and unpleasantness in black communities and among black people. Many black men have died in my stead. Many of them while profusely proclaiming their innocence, and many of them, while plainly innocent to officials and the public, are condemned for the dysfunction, on the matter of race, that takes place in the minds of white people. On many occasions, I've been accused of engaging in what they say is my favorite pastime, raping white women, a preeminent capital offense, and over the years scores of innocent black men have had to pay the price in the most horrific manner. Nothing ever enrages and blind the white man more than the accusation that I have bedded his woman—forcefully or not.

I don't mind that all white people describe me in the same way, after all, if they didn't, I could not exist. The energy of my existence comes from the imaginations of white people. It is through them that I derive my shape and form, my notoriety and malformation, my helplessness as well as my power. Yes, my power—although I have cast myself as a victim, on the Yang side of my weakness is my power, as on the Ying side of my power is my weakness. Slippery? Let me explain: This all happens in the collective white psychic. It is there that I am created. It is there that I am nourished and embellished. It is only there in the white mass psychic that I exist.

There was a time in the South when the majority of white voters favored the Democratic Party. During the civil rights era, the national Democratic Party aligned itself with the movement for equal rights, a move that alienated white Southerners, to whom my image became iconic for the Democratic Party—for them, an intolerable association. Over a period of three decades there was a massive shift of white voters to the Republican Party in order to keep the process of how best to retard the progress of black people clear. The irony is that this shift has resulted in millions of white people voting against their own self-interest, doing damage to their families, the political system, the country and themselves. The South is a region of the country where even professional people work a second and third job trying to make ends meet and yet, white people are persuaded to support policies that favor the rich, simply because they are certain these polices don't help blacks. Whenever they view the Democratic Party, they see that sketch of me and the distortion sends them off in the wrong direction. That is the kind of power they have given me. Admittedly, it's not a direct power I possess of my own accord, rather, a power that result from their folly—but power just the same.

Hold on tight—I am about to offer another concrete, but equally slippery observation: Much of what they do to prevent blacks from striving forward is also detrimental to many of them. It turns out that there is an inner-connectiveness between them. When they flock to the Republican Party in the hundreds of thousands to inoculate themselves of my presence, they also leave behind remedies to problems that afflict many of them. My power lies in their attempts to leave blacks out. For many of them, the solutions that would ease black burdens are the same ones that would bring them comfort. If a white man in the South, with two jobs, a working wife, three children, a double-wide trailer and a hunting dog would vote his reality he'd favor a reduction in his payroll taxes over a reduction in inheritance taxes. He'd seek a raise in the minimum wage and a membership in a labor union to protect his status, but because he is encouraged to associate these issues with my image, he rejects them and imprison himself on the outside of my cell thinking he's better off.

No one has accused me of any wrong doing in the recent wave of corporate scandals. This is in keeping with their propaganda that I am a dim-witted creature incapable of the kind of sleight of hand that robs millions of American workers of their future. They know that to draw a sketch of me in say, the Enron debacle, would be useless—white Americans would not believe it... without a sell. They believe much about me that involves mindless violence, but it would take a campaign to convince them that I am capable of financial thief and deception on such a grand and ruinous level. Such a capability requires a studiousness that begins in a quality grade school, a 3-point grade average in an Ivy League college, a facilitated acceptance in the corporate world and the ethics of Attila the Hun, who killed his brother Bleda, in the year 444, rather than share power. Attributes and preparations long denied to me.

Much will be said of my improved condition in this society when the day comes that my sketch appears in connection to grand scale corporate scandals—but that's like turning things inside out—a bad measure, or, perhaps, just a badly formulated way of seeing things. My world is measured in the negative. For an example, no one suspected me during the Maryland highway sniper horrors that killed many people. This is the work of white men even professional profilers were sure. A sketch of Leroy the Phantom Culprit is not practical in this case and would only lead to a delay in the apprehension of those really responsible for the shootings. In this case, it was thought, that a hunt for me would be a distraction that could cause the death toll to mount needlessly. We know who commits these heinous acts and it's not Leroy, the experts were confident. Well, now we know the results of that kind of thinking in this particular instance. Whether my elevation to mass murderer has validated my acceptance into the American family is still unclear. My progress is also measured in negative terms.

There, I have shared some of the high points in my recent existence with you, but I want you to know that I'm always on the job—operating on autopilot. When the clerk at the store interrupts waiting on a black person, to make eye contact with the next white person in the line, to give assurance that she will be served before the current customer is finished, that's the me in his head at work. When there's an altercation and the white policemen arrive on the scene and arrest the black victim and not the white perpetrator—I am alive. When the car dealer or realtor adds the hidden black tax to the deal, I toil in shrouded wakefulness. When local governments under fund schools in black areas, they invoke my presence. I'm manifested in various everyday means and it's these seemingly small symptoms that are my bloodline and my lifeline to the big headline times.

Although I've never been publicly exonerated once charged, and the truth later emerged. There had been times when, in the end, only the truth survived. The young white mother in South Carolina finally admitted to drowning her two sons and led the police to the gruesome site in the lake where their bodies lie clinging to each other in the back seat of her car submerged in the watery lie she told. Then they forgot about me and about the distress they caused in the black community in that area. And, the powerful New York politician made another more successful try for death that called off the search for me. The unfaithful husband in Boston finally ensnared by his lies, went back to that bridge and in his flight from it, perhaps, thought of joining his wife and the unborn son he didn't want, or the trouble he sent my way.

Now I look toward my long and eventful future with eagerness and anticipation. I never know when I'll be called upon again, only that I will indeed, *be called*.

TELEPATHIC GRAFFITI

If humans could hear me, here is what they would hear: Department store mannequins have lives...of sorts. And, which of you humans will dispute it? You humans debate whether the light goes out when the refrigerator door is closed. Humans don't know if a tree that falls in the forest makes a sound, if no human is there to hear it. So, don't pretend you know what we mannequins can, or can't do. Just sit down and put all your bias aside for a moment. Take it from one who knows. And, oh, how I know. I am, after all, the proverbial fly on the wall. Not only can I tell you about mannequins, but I also know about some mighty peculiar, human traits. I've seen it all. Anything you might image is said and done candidly in my presence. No human suspects that I am a conscious, cognitive entity. I and the other Mannequins at Regal's Department Store are often called dummies. "Put a full-bodied female dummy there," someone orders, "re-dress the top-half of that male dummy over there." Dummy, dummy, dummy. The humans who work around us and the humans, who shop here, are all unaware that we have visual and audio perception. It has something to do with the wires they use to hold our plastic molding together and how the heat of the body-molding machine affects the molecules and electrons in the wires. Knowing your view on the tree in the forest and the refrigerator light thing, I don't expect you to reach out and grasp this concept, at least, not yet. As I continue on, you will believe it, or not.

Anyway, the only ones among you who are suspicions of us are very young children. The younger they are, the more likely they are to suspect us of having some kind of an understanding and these young children sometimes try to communicate with us.

Once, a small boy got separated from his mother and wandered into the swim wear section of the store. It was early in the morning and there was one sales person there at the time. The boy cuddled up to xxff-411, who was sitting on a beach chair, under a large beach umbrella, with one foot on the floor and the other on a stool, both arms stretched out as though she was welcoming her young one from the water. The toddler was found leaning on xxff-411's lap comforted by the embracing arc of her lower arm, and trying, as best he could, to explain his case to the mannequin. This boy had a young mind still able to fancy all the possibilities. What a pity that humans often grow out of the intuitive wisdom they have as children. Grown humans go about their business oblivious to the fact that within we human-like figures, there is a light that doesn't go out and a sound that isn't heard.

One evening, I saw a man stuff three suits into an oversized bag. He kneeled low by the suit coffin furthest from the counter and stuffed his bag, out of sight of the salesman. I cried out thief, thief, but, of course, there was no response. Humans can't hear us. Mannequins see and hear everything, but there is no communication between man and mannequins. Mannequins communicate with each other on a telepathic wavelength created by the bizarre actions in our body wires, but we are not human. The thief filled his bag and eased away unseen by any human.

I am xxfm-213. I was shipped to Regal's store in the city of North Charleston, South Carolina, 7 years ago. At first, I was put in a display at the main entrance of the store. It was a family display with xxff-422, a small xxff, and a small xxfm. We were there every season for several years, dressed in the season's latest finery. The main entrance leads in from the mall and we were the first thing people saw when they came to Regal's. Making the right first impression was a grand responsibility and we performed magnificently for years. It was just recently that through some mix-up in redressing us that I was placed in the men's suit department. I stand at the entrance to the suit section wearing a pure wool, double-breasted, blue suit, by Hart, Schaffner & Marx. There are fifteen other mannequins scattered in the suit section, all wearing the very latest in fine men's tailored clothes. All together, there are forty mannequins in the men's department. There are no xxhf's or xxff's, only xxfm's and xxhm's. But there is a xxff in the alcove between the men's department and lingerie. She is xxff-435. She wears a pale pink see-through nightgown and she is looking good. In fact, all of the xxff's in Lingerie lounge around scantily clad in a variety of provocative poses. If mannequins felt erotic passion, xxhf-429 in Fragrance would own my heart. Had I one. She is only a top-half mannequin, which would make matters difficult, but what a face. The mannequin population at Regal's is around three hundred, including the ones in the stock rooms around the store, and the ones on the repair deck. We are everywhere.

Howard Beal and Tracy Christen work in the suit section. Beal is a retired man who worked on the railroads up north. He moved to Charleston and discovered he wanted to stay active, so he took this job selling suits. In his previous job, Beal received work-related benefits and he was treated as a valued part of the work force. He was in a big powerful labor union in his railroad job and that union protected him and his fellow workers from exploitation and provided a safe work environment. During those days Beal was sharp witted and kept a keen eye on his workers rights. The older Beal must have been lulled to sleep. The managers at Regal are taking him for a ride and he doesn't suspect a thing. He doesn't know that he was hired at two dollars under the company's minimum wage for his position. Or, that he worked a full year at a salary disadvantage. This, from a man with a full career of labor knowledge and experience. He recognizes the disparity between salaries in the two regions, but he hasn't extended this knowledge to his own situation. Howard Beal goes on for hours on end about the better working conditions in the north. About the south, he says, it's hard for a region with a history of free labor to be fair with its' paid work force.

Tracy Christen is a bright young man with a future somewhere in the world of literature. He is a Southern History buff from the coast of Virginia, spending a year in what he calls the real South. Tracy describes himself as a conservative who is against affirmative action, but he swelled with pride when he was given a large unearned pay raise. He approves the of "good-old-boy" network of advancement and advantage for some, but governmental attempts to right some old wrongs of others rubs him until he chafes.

Tracy comes from a working-class family. His father's views on race are manifested from this southern heritage, a lack of vision, and zero courage. These feelings were passed on from father to son. Tracy's feelings on race became conflicted during his college days, when he got to eat, live, study, and hangout with blacks. He learned some respect for the history and experience of black people in America. He played basketball, listened to jazz and hip-hop, and found his experience with black people a worthy one. Tracy got along swell with his black contemporaries, but according to his up bringing, this couldn't happen. Tracy is a true southerner and soon he had found his way back on track, racially speaking. Tracy plans to return to the University of North Carolina in the fall to work on his Masters Degree in American Literature. He is a redheaded temperamental man/boy who loves to read books and write his own poetry. Tracy and his fiancée, Mindy Brailfort took a small apartment in North Charleston last fall. She works in a coffee shop in the mall and is finishing up a culinary arts course.

Tracy once chased a shoplifter out of the door of the suit department, where a car and driver were waiting. The shoplifter jumped into the get-away-car and they nearly ran Tracy over. He returned to the suit department out of breath and with a renewed assessment of what his role needed to be if he was to remain safe in his job as a suit salesman. Tracy was hired at the going pay rate. The store's operations manager, who hired them both six months apart, knows that Beal doesn't know what happens to the light when the door is closed, and that Tracy is blessed by history, tradition, and the custom of the past three hundred years.

The operations manager is a woman named Cindy Cain. The workers call her CeCe to her face, but a host of other things behind her back. CeCe is the store manager's hatchet man. It is her job to keep the store's operations cost lean and low—a position she presides over with skill and relish. CeCe was trained to keep the store's operating cost at a minimum and at the years end she is thrown a bone in proportion to her success, or pay cut when she fails. The humans working here earn between five and eight dollars an hour. One hundred percent more than mannequins earn. The hours are long and the pay is low, so the staff is continually changing as people search for a job where they can earn a living wage. The workers at Regal's are a very unhappy lot; really like laboratory mice, running from one retail store to another. I once heard a worker lament "They pretend to pay me so I pretend to work." The complaints are endless and I often wonder why anyone would work here, but what else are they to do? None of the companies in the area offer any benefits beyond salary and there's no reason why they should in a region with an unorganized unprotected and exploited work force. Regal has three hundred stores throughout the South. They employ thousands of people at minimum wages, while their executives pull down huge salaries. They know all about the lights. I often wonder why anyone would work here, but what else can they to do?

Sadie Ann works directly across from the suit department. Sadie Ann is a saleswoman in the shoe department and she is a lip loose cannon. Life has dealt her a bad hand and she takes it out on her customers. A customer once complained to her about the price of a pair of shoes that he wanted to buy. Sadie Ann told him that if he couldn't afford to shop at Regal he should go to Wal-Mart. This is just an example of the mildest of her off colored comments to customers. There is no wonder that the customer complaints against her have piled high. Her bad hand involves her family back in the hills of Bale Creek, Kentucky and she lays the cards out with relish. When they have time between customers, the saleswoman and Beal stand across from each other and she tells him about her dysfunctional family back home. She has designs on Beal and oddly enough, she thinks that opening her family's jumbled closet to him...and unbeknownst by her, to the fly on the wall, is the way to win him over. Her family, she says, is dirt poor and illiterate. She grew up in the seventies in the family's old wooden house without running water or electricity. They had to go outside to use the toilet, but their poverty was typical so they didn't stand out from the other families on their side of the mountain. It wasn't until the mid-eighties that her family and some of the other families on the hill got indoor plumbing and electricity. By then, she, her husband and daughter, had left for South Carolina and an opportunity for a better life. The women in her family have a long history of internal hatred and abuse. Her great grandmother hated her grandmother, her grandmother hated her mother and her mother hates her. She comes from a family of five girls. She is her father's favorite and when she was a child, he often invited her to sleep with him and her mother. Her mother often abused her and she is convinced that her mother was jealous of the affection her father showed her.

There were no jobs in the area. They lived on what they could grow, and small monthly government checks. This is an area in the backwoods of Kentucky forgotten by God and man. There was a town forty-five miles away that had a mining company that provided some jobs, but none of the men from Bale Creek had the means or the desire to take advantage of this opportunity. They all piled into a truck once a month to go to town to buy staples and real whiskey. Many of the young adults who wanted something of a future left for brighter digs. Sadie Ann, her husband and daughter were, eventually, among them.

Sadie Ann is also convinced that her husband is in love with their daughter and his own sister. Since his sister followed them to Charleston, he has spent most weekends with her. He even vacations with his sister. He takes her to the honky-tonks to drink and listen to country music and, the shoe saleswoman is sure, it goes further than this. He spends far too much time alone with their daughter and has driven a wedge between daughter and mother. Lately her daughter has begun to act disrespectful towards her. In her despair she has come to the realization that she needs someone in her life. And, it is at this point in her exposé that she usually invites Howard to stop for drinks after work, an offer he politely postpones with, "Maybe one evening next week."

Meanwhile, back in the hills, she suspects her father who has been sickly for years now, is dying in a damp dark unkempt room. Her family has acquired a telephone, but whenever she calls they hang up on her when she asks to speak to her father. If her mother answers the phone she asked "What'a ya want? Ya whore," and hangs up. This saleswoman is a bitter, unpleasant person in her dealings with fellow workers and customers. Her rancor was sad for Howard and he would wince as she denounced her family and wished them ill fate. A few days ago, this loathsome creature got herself terminated. Her troubled life manifested itself once too often in her work. She is fortunate, however, that at Regal's, termination for humans doesn't mean the same as it does for mannequins...the shredding machine.

Mannequins experience no joy or gratification, but no sorrow or lamentation either. We are even keeled and without emotions. For most of the humans at Regal's, there is little of the former and much of the latter. The uncertainty and insecurity of their jobs keeps them on a perpetual emotional rollercoaster. They work long hours under oppressive work rules. They work nights and weekends at the same pay rate and have absolutely no say in how they are scheduled. They are expected to sell a hundred dollars of merchandise or more an hour. When they don't meet that expectation, they are fired without explanation or recourse. The morale is continually low and the workers whisper their genuine feelings to others that they trust and without knowing it, to the light that never goes out.

The manager of Regal's is a man name Karl Tross. He comes from an old southern Civil War family. He is unmarried and puts the whole of his life and the hole in his life into the operation of his store. To most of his employee's, he seems a pleasant easy going man but the few old timers still employed at the store know that this is because he has CeCe to make his hits. Karl Tross has nothing else in his life but the operation of his store. He isn't trying to reach upper management; this store is his path to the kingdom. On the work floor he is a deceitful fraud, who engages his workers in seemingly harmless, but calculated, small talk. His only concern is to operate his store under budget, and whenever the store goes off budget, CeCe hears from Tross. How this affects the workers is of no concern to CeCe or Tross, their main tool is fast worker turn over. This keeps the store from having long term employees who could earn salary increases. Having a warm body for every cash register is the goal. In a work force of eighty-five people, there are five that have been here more than five years. The average worker stays at Regal's five months, leaving before the second three-month review paycut. For Karl Tross, retail is war, in his mind his ruthlessness prevents the second burning of Charleston.

Xxff-123 overheard CeCe bringing a plan to Tross to oust a senior department manager whose salary, CeCe thought, had grown too large over time and was now a drag on the budget. They would assign her to a department, which was being phased out. Once the change was completed they would offer her a position as a sales associate, which CeCe had correctly calculated, the manager would not accept. Then once she was gone they would fill her position with an associate from the floor, at a much reduced salary rate. If a tree falls in the forest and there is no one there to hear it, does it take the drag off the budget?

Twice a week Tross holds store wide meetings. At these meetings, he gives pep talks to the staff and he hands out worthless prizes to that week's exceptional employees. "Betty in Handbags," Tross announces, "opened three new charge accounts," and with great fanfare, he gives her an empty watchcase amidst applauds from fellow employees. "Oh," Tross says, "BJ sold four thousand dollars yesterday." An empty shoe box for her. And on and on. At the end of these meetings, Tross always encourages everyone to have a good sales day and off they go. We mannequins are spared this curious generosity.

One day xxff-124 was accidentally knocked over and suffered a broken arm.

She was stored in a stockroom for a few days before she was taken to the loading dock for repairs. This is when she discovered that the stockroom was being used as a sex den. Each of the three days that xxff-124 awaited removal, Karen from customer service met Steve from Electronics in the tiny stockroom and they rolled around frantically on the merchandise. The third day, in their haste to make the most of a fifteen-minute break, they rolled over on xxff-124 and broke off her other arm. After being repaired, xxff-124 was placed in a window on the eastside of the building. Now she often boasts that she is the only mannequin in the store who has experienced sexual passion...of a sort.

Employees are told that there is no set profile for shoplifters. Anyone could be a shoplifter. Regal's employees are taught not to judge by appearance or race, but to be vigilante and courteous. But here is a curious thing that goes on in all the departments of the store. There is a group of thieves, two young white women, and two young black women who operate in all the departments of the store. They only do their business once they are all in the same department of the store.

The curious thing is this: When this gang of four get to their work site, they go into their act of not being together. The two white ones arrive first and browse around. Then the two black ones come into the department and this, by itself, catches the attention of the salespeople and any security people in the area. Now something magical happens. All eyes are on the black decoys. The blacks are watched and followed while their white conspirators go to work stuffing empty bags full with merchandise. This team of women knows what happens to the light when the refrigerator door in closed.

There are black mannequins and there are white mannequins in the store. This is to satisfy, what seems to us, some deep mystery in the human condition. Black, white, it makes no difference to us. We know that at the final count, we are all mannequins. There is a white human male who come into the store often. He has never let a black human serve him. When he is approached by a black salesperson, he moves on without a word. He won't even speak to a black salesperson. But rather grabs a white salesperson and demands to be rescued from the attention of that black person. Some curious behavior, indeed. But I'm convinced that this has something to do with why humans need black mannequins and white mannequins. We mannequins are black and we are white, by design, but there are no gay mannequins. There are, however, gay humans, several of them working right here at Regal's.

Gerry works in makeovers, and he is, as they say, very sweet. Gerry was once over heard telling a gay customer about a party he attended over the weekend. Gerry excitingly told the man about the food and the music, his hands waving wildly in the air as though he spoke with them. His face was filled with delight and he giggled uncontrollably as he whispered revelations about the dancing and all the interesting new men that flirted with him. Gerry extended the fingers of his left hand and touched the customer on his shoulder and the customer's eyes fluttered. Then Gerry brought his face close to the customer's to talk in secret. Both faces puffed red as Gerry told about the pairing and the late-night action. "Oh darling," Gerry concluded, " it was a deliciously scandalous affair."

There is an area in the mall where several gay men meet during the day to have lunch and socialize. One day an under aged boy made advances at Gerry while he and the others talked and ate. He returned from lunch that day to tell how he rejected the boy's overtures. He told the kid that he should find people his own age. Gerry was proud that the boy chose him from among the five or six gays in the crowd and that he could show them how he handled so tempting a situation. Strange as the human world is, it is queer that the gays who work at the mall seem to be the best adjusted and the happiest humans, all except for one. Billy Joe Carton is a young man of twenty-five, who is dissatisfied that his genes makes him operate with all the dispositions of a gay person. His walk and all of his movements are musically feminine. Although he has gone out with young males, there is a young girl who works at the store that he would like to date. This internal conflict has driven him to the psychiatrist's couch and daily doses of Prozac.

There is a rumor flying around the store that Karl Tross is to be transferred to another store in another state. This has brought hope and a brighter face to the employees. They are anticipating change, but I have heard one warn "be careful what you wish for, you may get it." But the hopes of a brighter future shines in their eyes. For humans there is always hope.

There is another rumor floating around. If I had emotions this would be a rather crushing and gloomy bit of gossip. Two large crates of mannequins are on the loading dock. State-of-the-art, rumor has it, more human looking then ever. The future is here. Time awaits no mannequin. At least I've had this time to lay out what I'd say to humans had I the ability to communicate with them. I'd tell them all of this and more. And, yes, I would tell them that the light goes out when the refrigerator door is closed, but I'm afraid, I have already asked them to believe too much.

THE DEVIL *BEATS HIS WIFE*

Y ou've all been summoned here to give testimony in the case of one J. Edgar Harrison, born August 8th 1934 in Charleston, South Carolina, died May 9th 2003. You have been brought together so that we may reconstruct the life of J. Edgar Harrison and that said life can be evaluated and a proper disposition and placement can be made. I commend you all for participating in the primary part of this inquest. It will, indeed, help to have you understand the process and procedure. We are here to gather the facts on the life of J. Edgar Harrison. You are, in essence, character witnesses for the applicant. Upon ascertaining all the pertinent details of his life, it will be my obligation to consider all of the testimonies and decide whether this matter moves to the next stage—which is a formal inquest before the full Beelzebub tribunal. If this matter reaches the full tribunal, some of you will be asked to appear before that chamber, depending on the importance of your testimony. Because what you say can weigh heavily on how this matter turns, I am duty bound to make you all aware that everything you say is important. Hold back nothing—there will be things that may seem insignificant to you, but this very same little thing can be the deciding issue in this process, so tell it all. Now I ask you to think long and carefully and not to filter anything out because you may think it doesn't matter.

"As you all know, J. Edgar Harrison was a complicated

human being. He was a controversial man who played many roles. He held positions in your school system, in your community, in your city and in your State Legislature. I will want to hear what you know about his conduct in these positions. He was a husband and a father. I want to know all there is to know about his behavior in this role. He was a lawyer and business partner. I want to know about his business dealings. He was a politician who's every position, it is alleged, has been contentious, malicious and loathsome. The evidence of this will have to come out through the testimonies given here. It states here on this application that he was a man who could spew hatred and teach Sunday school. It is also alleged that he was a man who never once tried to build anything up—he saw his role as destroyer. He made his contributions to society by tearing things down. You are the people who lived among him—you worked with him, you socialized with him, you worshipped with him, you planned and schemed with him, you shared life with him—you are the folks who knew him best.

"Now I will ask for your testimony. When the clerk calls your name, you will take the witness stand. You will begin by stating your full name, your relationship to the applicant, and the one word you would use to describe the applicant. If everything is understood—the clerk will now call the first witness."

"James Marvin McGee."

"You may take the witness stand and begin Mr. McGee."

"Jay was a sonabitch and..."

"Mr. McGee, would you please first state your full name and how it is you know the applicant."

"My name is James Marvin McGee. I grew up with J. Edgar Harrison and he was one sonabitch."

"You may refer to the applicant as Jay, Mr. McGee, if that's how you know him."

"Thank you sir, yes, I've called him Jay all of his life. We grew up together right here in the city of Charleston, went to law school together and later became partners in our own law firm. Jay comes from a family that has a long history in Charleston and the state of South Carolina. His great granddaddy fought in the Civil War, his granddaddy helped to dismantle reconstruction and institute Jim Crow laws that crippled Negro progress right up to this very day. His daddy fought long and hard to keep our lunch counters and schools segregated. This is the basic fabric that Jay springs from, but his family excelled and distinguished themselves in many other areas. There were charges of embezzlement, forgery, corruption and murder that followed the family for generations. This is the stuff that made J. Edgar Harrison what he was. And, sir, I was lucky to be so close to it all. I come from a ho-hum family of do-gooders, so I've got a perspective on the matter at hand, what I mean is—I can see both sides.

"I remember when we were little boys. We used to swim in the river under the bridge. Jay was always built kind of chunky—he was a big eater and kind of large for his age. Well back in those days we had to walk through a colored area to get to our swimming spot. A bunch of us boys would walk through the colored area thankful that they didn't jump us or something like that—not Jay, he would walk ahead of us spewing out the most spiteful assertions towards the people there, in a malicious tone and the foulest language. At eleven years old, Jay made it plain for all to know that he hated...well, it's a word we seldom use in public these days sir."

"Mr. McGee, in this forum, and for the purposes of these proceedings, you may, indeed you must, use the word."

"Well sir, at eleven years old, Jay made it known that he hated niggers—hated them enough to eat the hearts out of their living bodies and he spent his entire life proving that fact. Well, sir, on one hot summer day, we marched through the colored area, with Jay at the head of our column, much like Sherman marched through Charleston. A group of ...with your generous permission sir, a group of nigger boys was gathered playing something or another and when we reached them, Jay went to mouthing off with his venomous taunts. One little nigger boy jumped from out of the crowd of them—grabbed hold of Jay and beat the living shit out of him while the rest of us ran our scared asses off. That wasn't the end of that. Jay told Mr. Harrison, his daddy, how he got whipped by that nigger boy. Mr. Harrison found out through his network of niggers which boy rendered the whipping and where his family lived. Two nights later some men dressed in white sheets burned those folks home down—well two other homes burned down by the time the fire was put out, but these other two were not the intended target.

"That whipping only served to concentrate Jay's hatred. In the early fifties, when we were in our late teens, a bunch of us used to hang out on King Street on Saturday. We'd walk the streets, drink soda pop, go to the movies—that kind of thing. I remember one Saturday this nigger soldier comes strolling past us with his gal holding on his arm—a woman so fair skinned she might have been white. I believe this was somewhere near 1951 or '52. It was during the Korean War and the army had just been integrated for a few years. Jay was infuriated, hell I was mad too, but I could see from her features that she wasn't a white woman—she had full lips and too much rump to be a white woman. We were raging because President Truman integrated the army in 1948, before he left office in '52. Now to this nigger's mind, wearing the uniform of the United States Army gave him the privileges of a white man. This colored soldier thought he was good enough to parade down King Street with a near white looking woman on his arm. We weren't about to let a notion like that take hold. With all of us boys as backups, Jay taunted that nigger soldier from the sidewalk down to the gutter. We crowded around the soldier and his gal and Jay pushed them into the street where the cars traveled. Jay told him he wasn't good enough to walk on the same sidewalks with white people. Jay humiliated that boy while he was wearing the uniform of the United States army, right in front of his gal and the people who passed by—the gallant citizens of Charleston. That boy hurried his hide out of there lucky not to receive a whipping with his humiliation. Jay taught a lesson that day—even a nigger in the uniform of the United States army still gets treated like what he is—a nigger. We later heard that that boy was the son of a well-known and respected colored preacher from Charleston. The preacher complained to his local councilman and the incident was widely talked about around town, but that was all there was to it—except that a little colored national magazine named Jet, wrote up a whole page on the incident. Anyway, that preacher's son went off to fight in Korea and got himself shot full of holes on something called Porkchop Hill—this is when he made the newspapers in Charleston. Now sir, that's a repugnant story filled with some horrible ironies, but it is all the truth.

"As I said, Jay was always kind of chunky. When we entered Law school, he was wearing a size 44 suit. By the time we graduated, Jay wore a size 48. He was a big man and he intimidated people with his size and his mouth. I graduated number 94 in our class; Jay was number 90 in a class of 105. I passed the law examine on my first try. It took Jay 3 times before he passed the state bar—go figure? Anyway, when we got licensed, we tried working for other people, but we were new to the system plus, quite frankly sir, neither of us was much good at the law, so nobody employed us for very long. We stayed out of work more than anything else, so we finally teamed up. You ever heard that old lawyer's parable that says that any lawyer, who represents himself, has a fool for a client. When you apply that to Jay and I teaming up in a law firm, and need I say more? We found some cheap office space and hung our shingles on the door, so-to-speak. It took us a few years before we figured out how the system worked. One of us had to go into politics to funnel insider government information back to the other to grow the law firm.

"All of the positions in the State Legislature were filled each election by better known fellows from better positioned law firms than Harrison and McGee. Jay finally won a seat on the school board. It was a relatively small position, but we used the information Jay got back to me to build our law practice. For an example, Jay found out years in advance where new schools were needed. Our firm would buy up the land. Jay would promote and push the project and when the school board was ready to build a school, we'd sell them the land. Plus, we bought a small construction company and Jay got the school board to funnel the contracts to work on school construction projects to our company. Now we were getting the knack of how this lawyering thing works, and Jay was making enough noise to get noticed by the press and the forces of the status quo. There was a sizable group of retrogressionist in the state during those days and as they got to know Jay, they warmly welcomed him into their camp. By the time Jay got to the State Legislature, we were masters of duplicity, with families to support and big homes to maintain and lucrative contacts in state agencies.

"The South was changing though. Jay was like that little Dutch boy with his finger in the dyke trying to hold back the inevitable. The civil rights movement burst forth through the dam of retrogression with federal legislation after federal legislation. They desegregated public places and schools, and gave coloreds the right to vote—well you would think that it was all over for Jay, but it wasn't. Jay never spent a day in the military, but he was familiar with military tactics in a losing battle. Jay employed guerilla tactics to delay, confuse, confound and harass the enemy. And that was the kind of battle he waged for three decades. Jay gave them, if you will permit the expression sir, hell. Up until the hour he died, Jay was plotting ways to defeat a school bond to raise funds to support and improve education in the area. Life for black people and for the people of South Carolina generally, would have been a sight different if it weren't for the nasty works of J. Edgar Harrison. He was a man who saw his duty and got great pleasure doing it. Jay was a sonabitch, and I've told it like it was. That's all I have to say about that."

"Thank you Mr. McGee. You may return to your seat. Will the clerk call the next witness."

"Miss Abergale Brooks."

"Miss Brooks to the stand please."

"My name is Abergale Ann Brooks and I served for ten years on the school board with Mr. Harrison. When I think of Mr. J. Edgar Harrison the one word what comes to mind is obstructionist. He was a champion of the status quo and a man of such foul hatred it will take him 6000 lifetimes to reach nirvana. I pray that in his next life he will be a thing of some neutrality—maybe a tree or a flower. Yes, a flower, for a flower gives freely of its fragrance without the will to pick and choose who receives it. But, I fear, even that won't do, for there isn't any nobility in doing good if one does not have the free will to do the opposite, but still chooses doing good. And Mr. Harrison needs badly to score some good points in his next life. If in his next life he is granted free will and uses it the way he has in his last life, he may not obtain nirvana in a million years—what misery. Sir, before I say anything about my dealings with Mr. Harrison, I insist on saying a prayer for his soul."

"This kind of thing is highly unusual here Miss Brooks, it just simply has never been done, but I find the prospects for being amused irresistible—proceed."

"Open up your heart
And see that Buddha
Smiles within."

"Now your testimony Miss Brooks."

"Besides serving on the school board, I am the director of our library system. One of my responsibilities is to procure books for all the libraries in the system. I read profusely. I write proficiently. I know the importance of the written word to the developing mind. I served on the school board because this is where I could best utilize my expertise. Books, my dear sir, are paramount to the growth of the whole human intellect; mind, spirit and body. While I was on the school board, I tried constantly to keep our textbooks up to date. This requires money, but if we are going to educate our children properly—it's money well spent. Mr. Harrison opposed my every effort. I explained to him that in some of our schools the children were using science textbooks that were eight years behind the times. In the late eighties, our children were using science books that made no mention of the great advances in computer technology. It was Mr. Harrison's opinion that the children in private schools would be the leaders of future society and if they were getting a good education, the children in public school shouldn't cost the taxpayers too much money. Mr. Harrison really didn't believe in the system of free public schools and was trying to destroy it from within.

"Some of us on the school board recognized the need to create programs that would integrate undisruptive special needs children into regular classrooms. It required some special training for our teachers, but the payoff for the children in self-esteem and community pride would have been enormous. Sir, this would have been a program that would have benefited all the children. This early association with special needs children would make the so-called normal children more tolerant to differences in other people they met as they grow up. This was something good. If there were more magnanimity among people, it would lower your workload."

"Thank you for your concern Miss Brooks, but I rather enjoy my work and welcome a heavy case load. You may continue."

"He obstructed this program—calling it unnecessary and too costly. He objected to putting what he called normal kids in the same classrooms with retarded zombies. He was wickedly blunt. He had his followers on the school board and he threatened to expose the wasteful improprieties of those who disagreed with him to the taxpayers and voters. Mr. Harrison knew how to make a headline and he had his allies in the media, so a majority of the school board members went along with him.

"Many African-American parents noticed that their children weren't receiving a satisfactory education and started to campaign to get some of their own on the school board. We had an At-Large system of election for school board members back then. This was designed specifically to keep them off of the board. The general district population elected all of the board members. Under this system, African-Americans didn't have enough votes to elect one of their own to the board. In order to give some African-Americans a chance to get elected, the entire school system would have to be broken up into individual districts. This would have to be acted on by the State Legislature, but Mr. Harrison lobbied the lawmakers and they refused to create voting districts in the school system. They wantonly attempted to keep people off the board whose children made up a majority of the students in the system. To Mr. Harrison, the mission of a school board member was to keep the cost of a public education low, and not that of representing the children's educational needs. The issue had to be settled by the United States Justice Department. Sir, for decades our children's test scores fell behind the test scores of children in most all of the other states, thanks to this evil obstructionist. I don't wish his application any success here, but he may have earned it."

"Thank you Miss Brooks, you may step down. Clerk, next witness, please."

"Mr. Ned Neilson."

"Mr. Neilson, you may take the witness stand."

"My name is Ned Neilson. I'm a writer, a social and political commentator and a radio personality. It's through these capacities that I have come to know and cover J. Edgar Harrison. The word that comes to mind when thinking about Jay Edgar is bigot, but I've called him worse. I'm not Southern—you may have deduced that from the fact that I only have two names. I moved here from the North, twenty-three years ago. I was trying to break into the radio business up in the North, but there are just too many talented people up there. I was a little white fish in a big white pond—here, my abilities shine over them all. I'm a little white fish in a little white pond—but here, I'm also a Jew.

"Look, there are a million racists in South Carolina, tens of millions in the South generally and maybe a hundred million in the United States and some of them are black. Jay Edgar and five or ten others in this state, are in the forefront of the movement. You would have to look deeply into conservative enclaves in the federal government to find racist as blatant and creative as Jay Edgar and his Low Country pals. I once attended a fund raising breakfast as a guest journalist. The breakfast was attended by a clannish group of two hundred right-wing political activists. Slave master Jay, that's what I normally call him, Sla'Master Jay was one of the featured speakers. He started his speech off by laying out all that society was doing to try to help the black man and he enumerated a lengthy list. 'But let me tell you my friends,' Sla'Master Jay said at one point during his speech, 'all a colored man needs is tight poontang, loose shoes, and a dry place to shit.' He got a tremendous laugh out of that one. Then he went on to say some really racist things. And, he wasn't too kind to Jews either, although he knew that I was there to report on the event. He told the one about the guy who thought he'd get out of making a payment to a Jewish merchant by trying to pay him on Saturday, the Jewish Sabbath. He knew that the Jew wouldn't touch money on the Sabbath, so he went to the merchant's shop on a Saturday to offer the payment, only to be instructed by the Jew, determined not to let any money pass him by, to—'Leave it on the counter.'

"On the racial front, there is in this state what I call the axis of idiocy. This consists of five or ten highly visible politicians, some editorial writers and opinion makers in the media and the unseen hand of the oligarchy. The editorial writers and the media opinion makers, through sometimes subliminal means, but most often through overt means, suggest to the mass white population that the minority community is getting more out of society than they deserve, and that this some how short changes them. The politicians reflect and reinforce this view in the legislation that they enact. And, the unseen hand of the aristocracy orchestrates all of this to its own benefit. Although I refer to them as the axis of idiocy, their plan works brilliantly in keeping common people at each other's throat and the ruling class at the helm. It does nothing for the advancement of society and race relations, and in the final analysis, anything that doesn't work toward the advancement of society is obstinate folly."

"Mr. Neilson, I would remind you to restrict your testimony to the specific dealings of the applicant in this case—one J. Edgar Harrison."

" Sir, I was attempting to give you the big picture—to kind of show you the waters and the other creatures in the waters in which Sla'Master Jay swam."

"Mr. Neilson, my ruling will be based solely on the deeds of the applicant—not his environment or the deeds of his cohorts. Everyone reaches this place on his or her own merits. Please continue with this in mind."

" Some people can draw as much self satisfaction from doing an evil deed as others get out of benevolence –Sla'Master Jay was one such person. He was good at being mean, destructive and evil and this brought a sense of accomplishment and well being to Sla'Master Jay. It made him feel like he was master of his universe and all within its sphere. Sir, there is a huge number of white people in this state and in the South generally, with chips on their shoulders stemming back from the Civil War. In one way, these chips are similar to computer chips—they have long time memory. It's a grudge that's been past down from generation to generation since 1865.

"Now stick with me for a minute. Contemporary Southerners know from today's realities that the North winning the Civil War was the best outcome. Consider for a moment the consequences had the South won its independence from America. No one can calculate the changes this would have brought to the past 150 years of North American history. This animosity they hold for their conquerors is permanently imbedded in them, but it is most often directed at the victims of that past history—African Americans. Sure Southerners hate New York, but it's black people they discriminated against. Now Sla'Master Jay and his kind know how to tap into that centuries old resentment. That's what the Jim Crow period was all about—with the separate drinking fountains and public facilities. This was a means of keeping that resentment stoked. Now, with all of that gone and done away with, Sla'Master Jay and his crowd evoke that old resentment with the last vantage of the Old South—the Confederate flag.

"The Confederate flag is the last stand for Sla'Master Jay and all the overt bigots of South Carolina—but it's also the last stand for lots of poorly educated unsophisticated common white folks who are easily manipulated. The truth is this: these folks have more in common with ordinary black people than what separates them. The socio-economic position of both groups would be improved were they to join together politically—but here is where the bluebloods perform their slight-of-hand. The bluebloods wants to keep the two groups apart, so it tricks the white working class and white poor voters into continually voting their aspirations and not their realities. Poor and working class white people see their whiteness as their pass to riches. They think that they got all it takes to become rich –whiteness, so they vote for policies that benefit the wealthy for the day when they fulfill their whiteness.

Why else would a poor redneck who lives in a trailer home, has a wife and three kids and works two jobs that pays so little he still qualifies for food stamps, prefer a decease in the inheritance tax over a decrease in the payroll tax? Because he's got Sla'Master Jay and his gang, pulling the strings of his mind on behalf of the oligarchy.

"Most people think that Sla'Master Jay's obstructions only hurt black people, but that's not true. It's plain to see that this man was damaging to white people and to society as a whole and that is true evil. Isn't that what this inquest is about—thank you."

"I thank you Mr. Neilson. Clerk."

"Colonel Harvey Byron Williamson."

"Colonel Williamson take the stand."

"My name is Harvey Byron Williamson. I am a member of the South Carolina State Senate. J. Edgar Harrison and I were allies in that august body. We were also members of the Sons of the Confederate, from whence my title of Colonel comes. It is a wholly honorary title, but one that I cherish even more than the title of Senator Williamson. The one word that comes to mind thinking about my dear collaborator is rebel. He was a true Southerner for all the ages. Senator Harrison was so attuned to the temperament of the white South that he was as much a part of the South of 150 years ago as he was a part of the current South. He had the spirit of Johnny Reb and a real dedication to the traditions of the South. He was a defender of the Southern way of life.

"We met in the State Senate chambers and allied ourselves in the fight to keep blacks out of politics and especially out of the senate and the government. We lost that one, but as we got them on the floor of the senate, we gave them a psychological hazing and ignored any effort they made to offer legislation.

Yes, sir, we gave those black politicians the blazes—if we had slop buckets, we would have made them take them out. They haven't passed ten pieces of meaningful legislation over the 30 years that they have been serving in the State Legislature. We kill most of their bills in committee and when they manage to get one to the floor, we vote it down. They don't chair a single committee of importance. Our forces defeated the Hate Crimes bill that would have given homosexuals, coloreds and other minorities more protection from the law than white heterosexuals. We tried to keep Mexicans out of South Carolina until we recognized that they are a source of cheap labor. Sir, I respectfully submit to you today that there is but one man responsible for the success we've had in keeping the tradition of the South strong and the nigger politician in his place, he is J. Edgar Harrison.

"Senator Harrison frustrated them at every turn—to the point that one black senator offered him outside to slug it out. Senator Harrison had killed his piece of legislation just for the heck of it and to keep them from getting credit for doing anything consequential. Senator Harrison didn't accept the offer. Now the South Carolina Legislature has a long history of vendetta's that developed into violent resolutions, and in the old days, even shoot-outs, but Senator Harrison wasn't about to give a nigger senator such an honor. You see, these kinds of involvement make legends.

"We have lost an important gatekeeper in the senate and an important soldier in the Sons of the Confederate, for which he played such a crucial role. He was our liaison officer with other Southern orientated organizations. His office coordinated the concerted action of the anti-civil rights establishment. J. Edgar Harrison was a man dedicated to the supremacy of the white race and it is in his spirit that we shall carry on."

"Thank you Colonel. You may step down. I see that we have gone well past noon. Perhaps this would be a good time to have a recess. Clerk, how many more witnesses do we have?"

"Three, sir."

"Alright then, we'll press on. Call the next witness."

"J.C. Pinkney."

"Mr. Pinkney, please take the stand."

"It's Senator Pinkney, or Reverend Pinkney, sir."

"Senator Pinkney, take the stand."

"My name is J.C. Pinkney and I served in the State Senate with J. Edgar Harrison. The word that comes to my mind for Harrison is crafty. He was a crafty parliamentarian, but he was motivated by hatred. I can imagine the good he could have done as clever a man as he was in getting people to go along with him. He could have been a great man had he used his talent in the opposite direction. He could have avoided having this review that could land his soul in the netherworld. And much as that man abused and maligned my people, I am here to testify for the redemption of his soul."

"Senator Pinkney, you're a preacher?"

"Yes sir, A Baptist Minister."

"I will have to remind you, as I did Mr. Neilson, that I am solely interested in the deeds of the applicant and not anyone's assessment of the disposition of the applicant's soul. In other words, don't preach to me."

"J. Edgar Harrison worked for the devil all his days on earth and some will say that he ought to reside with the devil for all eternity. That he has earned the devil's acceptance, and that this application passes all the standards to get to the gates of hell. J. Edgar Harrison was a bad man, an evil man without a drop of tolerance or compassion for his fellow man. Yes, J. Edgar Harrison squandered his life away in hatred and destruction, incrimination and hostility, belligerence and cruelty. When it rains and the sun is shining, we say that the devil is beating his wife and that's the way it was in every day of this man's life. The sun shined, but the devil beat his wife, trying to put a damper on God's Grace. But as you well know God infused the flame of righteousness and the flame of evil into every man and every woman. And in the middle of the flames, He placed the freedom of will—the freedom to choose. And, in the course of a lifetime, we sometimes choose righteousness and we sometimes choose evil. And, the scale that weighs our morality shifts back and forth, as each tries to diminish the other. Evil only wins a soul when it can completely diminish the flame of righteousness, not when it has worn it down to a tiny flicker. Sir, I respectfully submit to you that there still was in J. Edgar Harrison an intermittent flicker of righteousness that existed at the time of his death. Oh yes, evil was in control for the entire length of his life, but evil never once completely conquered his spirit of righteousness. His flame of righteousness was not completely diminished. And if you are a representative of the devil, you would know that there ain't ever been a soul with even the tiniest spark of righteousness left in it, which is all J. Edgar Harrison had, admitted into hell—no matter how often the devil beats his wife.

"Sir, J. Edgar Harrison had a wife and family—he must have loved them and it must have been that love that kept a spark of righteousness burning in his life. Although, everybody else, friends and foe, saw him as he was, an odious human being, his family must have seen the spark. I refuse to believe that a man can have a wife and raise a family and not possess a spark of decency."

"Senator, Senator, Reverend Pinkney, I have asked you not to preach to me. The facts, my good man the facts and only the facts. Is that clear?"

"I have no apology to make sir, for I am moved by God the Almighty to speak on behalf of the applicant's salvation. If I can forgive him on behalf of all of my people, the people he antagonized all his life, and point out to you that there was still a flicker of decency in him—then you can't have him. You lose a soul because God reigns—God reigns."

"Clerk, call the next witness. Step down preacher, step down."

"Mrs. Nora Mae Harrison."

"Mrs. Harrison, please take the stand."

"My name is Nora Mae Harrison. I am the wife of J. Edgar Harrison. My husband was a domineering man. Domineering…"

Mrs. Harrison, you will have to speak louder."

"Yes sir, domineering is how I would describe my husband. We started seeing each other after he finished law school, but our families have known each other for over a century. We didn't fall in love and marry, but was sort of thrust into matrimony by arrangement and tradition. Our families arranged our marriage, not in any overt way as they did in ancient times, but more as of a merger of convenience and maybe that is why Jay has never been able to show me or our two sons any tenderness. He has been a man too involved in our family's mission—hatred, to give a little love and affection to his wife and sons. The night our first son was born, he ran off for a meeting with the Concerned Citizen's Committee up in Columbia. He said that the meeting was of high importance and was in the works for several weeks. Well, our baby was also of high importance and it had been in the works for nine months. This is a typical story through all the years that we were married. Jay got caught up in making other people's lives miserable at a very young age and all his life he derived such heinous pleasure from it.

" Jay witnessed his first lynching in 1947, when he was just 13 years old. People were standing around the lynched body drinking soda pop and eating pigskins like it was half time at a football game. There was so much gaiety among the people that it gave the event an atmosphere of normality. So, he grew up thinking that there was nothing that would be wrong to do against coloreds. He had witnessed the ultimate with a soda pop in his hand. You expose a young impressionable white Southern boy to the notion that coloreds are expendable, given the history of the South, and what you get is the man that Jay turned out to be.

"To tell the truth, I have always been jealous of the attention the Negro people received from Jay. Not the type of attention mind you, but rather, the amount of attention. It was almost as though he was in love with them. He devoted his entire life to delivering their grief. I guess you would say he was obsessed with them. I wanted some of that time. His sons wanted some of that time. There was a period when I thought that if I worked with him, sharing in his passion and got him used to me working at his side in his endeavors that I would be able to slowly steal some of his time for normal family activities, but that never materialized. It was like he had blinders on; absolutely nothing could distract him from his mission of making people's lives miserable. That was what he lived for and why he lived. Ours was not, in any manner, a healthy marriage. The more liberal the country became on matters of race, the more Jay stuck out from the norm, this didn't make being related to him easy for me and our sons. We were the brunt of ridicule and jokes. I turned to food for gratification, our sons turned inward and later to drugs and alcohol. Jay ruined the lives of many black people by giving them all of his time and attention. He ruined the lives of his own family by not giving us any of his time or attention. Now you tell me, whom did he love most?"

"Thank you Mrs. Harrison. Clerk, call the final witness."

"Ms. Tangerine Haverwhite."

"Ms. Haverwhite to the witness stand."

"My name is Tangerine Anne Haverwhite. I am the illegitimate daughter of the applicant, or so my mother told me. I never met Mr. Harrison, but the word that I would use to describe him is hypocrite. My mother used to work for the Harrison family back in the late fifties. Mr. Harrison forced my mother to have sex with him on several occasions and when she became pregnant with me, he made her go away. My mother moved to Pittsburgh, Pennsylvania, months before I was born. He hated black people, but not too much to lie down with one, or maybe even that was an expression of his hatred. Anyway, he paid my mother for her silence and she used the money to educate me. She remained for all of her days a woman tormented by the stigma of her past.

"There was always this unseen thing, this, this unseen gloom that hovered above us. I could never explain it, but it seemed my mother was always on the verge of telling me something—some big dark secret. There was something mysterious about the two of us, but only half of us knew what it was. My mother never married or knew many men. She put her life into mine up until the day she died—and it was only then that she disclosed the awful truth to me "

"Died. What was your mother's name?"

"Anne Bell Haverwhite, Sir"

"Clerk, give me a report on that name"

"Done sir, we have no record of her. She went the other way."

"You may continue Ms. Haverwhite."

"I have nothing else to say. Everything I know is hearsay. I know nothing about the man who was my father."

"You may step down. I want to thank you all for your testimony. You may go to lunch. We will reconvene in two hours for the decision."

Two hours later:

"All stand."

"You may be seated. I trust you've all had a hot lunch. I want to once again thank you all for coming forward with your testimonies. I have heard all the facts as they pertain to this case and I have weighed them accordingly. It has been demonstrated that the applicant did his utmost to qualify for residency in the infernal abyss. I delighted in hearing the exploits of this man's efforts to sabotage God's Grace. Alas, it has been pointed out, abundantly clear, I might add, that at the time of his death, there was still left in the applicant's heart, a tiny flicker of righteousness. Application denied."

THE BLACK FREIGHTER

Toots Jenny stood in the attic window circling her kerosene lamp as she had done every night since Luis Miguel Matos said farewell. She was sending her signal out to sea. She made two wide-arching circles, then two small circles. Toots Jenny alternated the size of the circles and repeated them over again. The motion created a gyrating effect, that in the darken night, would be easily sighted miles out beyond the mouth of the inlet. This is just how Luis Miguel had instructed her to do it. Toots Jenny had circled her lamp for so many nights now it had become an empty exercise of habit. An hour later she went to bed.   Toots Jenny was a slave owned by the Bouchet brothers. She was a scrubber woman in the family's hotel that was built on an inlet near Beaufort, South Carolina. Laurent and Travis Bouchet built the first ten-room Hideaway Tavern and Inn nearly two decades before the start of the Civil War. The Bouchets were fugitive pirates hiding from New Orleans authorities. In April of Eighteen Forty-two, just hours before they would have been arrested, the brothers abandoned their crew and fled to South Carolina, with four slaves and a freeman cook. The pirate brothers were familiar with the many inlets in the Port Royal Sound area on the lower coast of South Carolina. It was a secluded and seldom-traveled section of the coast that they used to evade authorities on many occasions. It took nine months and three clandestine trips back into New Orleans by Laurent Bouchet, the older of the brothers, to transfer their wealth and valuables to their new home on the inlet. On his final foray back into New Orleans, Laurent Bouchet also brought back his half breed common-law wife. Her name was Bentra Renear and she was of French and Indian lineage. She was a tall thin woman, who was as dark as her Indian mother and as audacious as her rouge French father. Once after a particularly violent fight, she cut off a joint of Laurent Bouchet's pinky while he slept. The Bouchets were both short stocky built men with hairy bodies. They came from French ancestry. They were both cunning and resourceful, but in all their dealings, Laurent was clearly the leader. They built the Hideaway Inn on the right side of an inlet that fed in from the Broad River. From Laurent's trips back among the underworld of New Orleans, word spread about the safe haven the Bouchet Brothers had established. In a year the Hideaway Inn became a popular spot for notorious pirates and land bandits of every stripe. The place flourished before the start of the war because it was the perfect spot for bandits on the run. As word spread farther among the underworld about the Bouchet's safe haven off the coast, it became difficult for the brothers to accommodate all the transitory bandits and fugitives who came for a stay. The brothers built a second ten-room building behind the first. And, even these rooms quickly filled with bandits. The Bouchets found themselves understaffed for all the chores that needed to be done. Two of the slaves that accompanied the brothers to the inlet died shortly after the second building was finished. Still, the garden had to be cultivated. Meals had to be cooked and served. Rooms had to be cleaned. Clothes had to be washed. Floors had to be scrubbed. Laurent and Travis Bouchet understood that this problem was as much a sign of their success as the cash that flowed into their chest.

Travis Bouchet went to a tobacco planter in Beaufort where he purchased five slaves. Two females in their thirties, twelve year old Jenny and two sickly ten-year-old boys whom the planter deemed unsuitable for work in the tobacco fields. Travis paid the going price for the two women. He got the boys for what he considered a good price, but he paid dearly for Jenny who was strong and healthy. The two boys wailed away at being separated from their mothers and siblings and the familiarity of the only life they knew. The women showed little emotion. Jenny went passively, her rage hidden inside her chest. She had lived a short life that had taught her not to expect anything but hardship. Adversity surrounded everything she knew of black life. Travis thought her attitude admirable. On the walk back to the Hideaway Inn, he called her "Toots" a term used in his circle to express esteem. Jenny was given a room in the attic of the two-story main building so she would be readily available. The main building had a veranda that ran around the second floor that provided a view of the inlet. From the attic window, the mouth of the inlet could be seen. The rear building was plain and had few windows. The two women were assigned to the main building. One of the boys was assigned to the freeman cook, and the other to the rear building. They were all given assignments and regular chores, but they did whatever they were told. Thus began the second stage of Jenny's life away from the tobacco plantation. She grew up serving the many rugged and notorious figures who called out to "Toots" Jenny, and in time the name stuck.

Toots Jenny served their meals, washed their plates, emptied their night pots, scrubbed the floors, made the beds, and counted their heads. The latter activity started after she met Luis and was, of course, unknown to anyone. The Hideaway Inn continued to be a busy safe respite for criminals who came and went on an impulse. There were always large groups of men hiding out from the authorities, or just lying low between jobs. People in the surrounding areas, including the town of Beaufort, knew about the villain-infested Hideaway Inn, but few spoke about it—some out of fear and others merely thought it was no business of theirs. These were rowdy rouges of the lowest kind; men who would slit a throat with hardly an interruption to their breakfast. The Hideaway Inn had a makeshift casino room where the men drank and gambled. Whores from nearby towns were brought in on wagons. The men were nearly always drunk and brawling. Several men had been killed there over the years and buried unceremoniously off the marsh to the side of the rear building. They spoke a language suitable only for hell itself. They spat at Toots Jenny and called her foul names. She emptied their night-pots and took their abuse with only a grumble.

Travis Bouchet treated Toots Jenny as a slave on most days. And, there were times when in drunken induced lust, he would visit her in the attic and force himself on her. This started when Toots Jenny was fifteen and fully developed. In all of her fifteen years of life, trouble and hardship was all she knew. Early on, back in her days at the tobacco plantation, the suffering and the suffocating mood of hopelessness triggered in her a detachment from the *nowness* of her reality. Her mental capacity was completely overwhelmed by her reality. She was hollow and empty and lived in a space that rejected the present. All of those many nights in the attic when Travis Bouchet thrust his drunken body against hers, for Toots Jenny, it was another chore, the worse of her many chores. When she was sixteen, she gave birth to a baby boy. She named him Moses and for a brief moment she allowed herself the danger of owning an emotion.

When Toots Jenny was nineteen, a crew from a Spanish ship rowed a landing boat up to the hotel pier. The ship was the Black Freighter. It carried sugar from Cuba that was headed for a merchant in Charleston and a contraband satchel of gold and jewelry from Mexico that was not listed on the ship's manifest. There were eight men in the landing boat. There was one black man amongst them. His name was Luis Miguel Matos. He was dark as night, with white teeth and a lean chiseled body. Luis was twenty-three years old and the youngest member of the crew. Luis Miguel was born in Cuba on the plantation of Don Carlos Miguel Matos, a minister in the government of Spain and governor of the Spanish colony of Cuba. Don Carlos employed two hundred ex-slaves and owned the largest sugar plantation in Cuba. Luis Miguel was a bright boy. He worked himself out of the sugar cane fields and into the home of Don Carlos as a servant. There—Don Carlos took notice of the boy's adeptness and allowed him to be educated. When he was fifteen, Luis Miguel was leased to a Spanish cargo ship as a cabin boy to learn the profession of sailing. On his seventeenth birthday, Luis Miguel was made a citizen of Spain. He was given a commission in the Spanish navy and spent all of his young years sailing the seas of the Americas under the Spanish flag. Luis Miguel was the pilot of the ship now anchored in the deep waters off the mouth of the inlet to the Hideaway Inn.

Toots Jenny spotted Luis Miguel right off as the men filed into the tavern speaking in broken English that she had never heard before. Luis Miguel carried himself with ease and he seemed, to Toots Jenny, to be the equal of the white Spaniards with him. They laughed and patted each other on the back. After they were seated, Toots Jenny saw the dark one issue what appeared to be an order to the one who went to fetch the whiskey. There was a party of pirates at the table near the kitchen door. They had been there eating and drinking for an hour. A member of the group was returning from the kitchen with another serving of mustard greens, yams, and chunks of fried pork with the rind, when a drunk and playful shipmate tripped him. The man fell to the floor. His face landed in the tin plate and the hot pork grease that was put on the yams burned him. A brawl broke out that lasted a few minutes and ended with an outburst of laughter. The short squabble left spilled food and an overturned wooden bench.

"Git ov'r heah and set dis mess right," the playful pirate called out to Toots Jenny, who stood hypnotized by the group of Spaniards, particularly the black one, and didn't move right away. The man who had been tripped took out a dagger and hurled it at Toots Jenny. "Git moving ya black creature," his words scored a more direct hit than his dagger, which fell harmlessly to the right of where Toots Jenny finished scrubbing up another mess. The dark Spaniard slammed his drinking tin to the table and attempted to rise to Toots Jenny's defense, but was held back by a wiser member of his group. Toots Jenny scurried over and began to work. Under the watchful eyes of the rowdies, who had moved to another table, Luis Miguel walked over to help Toots Jenny turn the wooden bench upright. As they bent to lift the bench, Luis Miguel's eyes met with those of Toots Jenny. She was touched by his kind act and impressed with his bravery. She nodded her thanks and her eyes bared a silent communication. The entire history of her misery was revealed to Luis in the instant of her stare. Luis had the kind of experience to understand every nuance of her communication, and with his eyes he conveyed his commiseration. Luis sent a mocking look towards the drunken men, who remained unprovoked, then he returned to his group. The leader of the Spanish boat party spoke with Laurent Bouchet to arrange a three-day stay for his group. The Spanish ship Captain told Laurent Bouchet about the sugar cane laden ship at the mouth of the inlet, but said nothing about the contraband his ship carried.

Luis Miguel watched Toots Jenny with interest as she worked about the Inn during the day. The nights after the incident, Luis Miguel came to her room in the attic. It was far past midnight. Toots Jenny and her three year old son Moses, slept on straw bedding, her by the door, he under the window. Toots Jenny wasn't surprised to receive this visit, it was, in fact, a visit she expected. Toots Jenny nodded for Luis Miguel to sit in the chair next to her straw mattress. Luis Miguel, who spoke fluent Spanish and French, struggled with English as he tried to talk to Toots Jenny. He told Toots Jenny about his days working in the cane field in Cuba. He told her that he had witnessed the cruelty of slavery in Cuba, French Guiana, Guyana, Surinam, Brazil and the islands of the Caribbean, all of which were places he had been during his travels. Luis Miguel talked about a place called Haiti where Toussaint L'Ouverture, a black general and liberator, defeated the British and then the French to free the slaves and established an independent black nation. Toots Jenny only understood the tone of what was being said, partly because of Luis Miguel's poor English and partly because it all seemed too unfamiliar and unfathomable.

Luis Miguel didn't say anything for a while. Toots Jenny stared up at him, a puzzled look on her face. She reached her hands out to him. He grabbed her hands and fell onto the mattress in an eager embrace. And, for the first time, what she had only known as a chore suddenly had meaning and pleasure. Before he returned to his quarters, Luis Miguel told

Toots Jenny that like General L'Ouverture, he would one-day return to liberate her. Then he showed her how to signal with the kerosene lamp. Toots Jenny began sending out her signal just weeks after Luis Miguel Matos and his crew rowed back to their ship and sailed off over the horizon.

In all, Toots Jenny gave birth to five bastard sons who were all sold off at an early age. Toots Jenny was never a beautiful woman, but she was once a woman whose youthful female figure excited desires in the rouges at the Hideaway Inn. This brought additional misery upon her. Her first son was born when she was sixteen and the fifth and last son was born when she was twenty-four. All were conceived from forced situations. Then fate stepped in to do something inside of Toots Jenny's body that prevented her from ever conceiving again. Through the miracle of motherhood, Toots Jenny felt some maternal instincts. She loved each of her sons and she hated each of her sons. She hated that proportion of each son that was comprised of the rapist who fathered him. She hated each for coming into a situation that deepened her agony. She didn't know where her love for each son came from...or why?

It was four years after her first son Moses, was born, that an outlaw she knew only as Bart fathered her second son. She named him Luis, for the dark Spaniard that she, at the time hoped would come to rescue her and her two sons. She could only guess as to the identity of her third son's father. She named him Luke. Her fourth son, whose birth almost killed her, was named John.

Travis Bouchet viewed even the product of his own sperm as property. While Toots Jenny was pregnant with her fifth child, Travis Bouchet, who was its father, sold Moses to the same tobacco planter from whom he had years earlier purchased Jenny. When the fifth son was born, Toots Jenny named him

Moses, as if to replace the sold boy. In an absurd twist of logic, some years later, Travis Bouchet sold the younger Moses to the same planter. He felt that the least he could do was to keep the two boys connected. This eased his conscience, such as he had. Then the other three boys were each sold a year apart from each other. By the age of thirty, all of her sons had been sold off. She was alone again. Toots Jenny grew large, ugly, and demented.

Jenny first heard about God on the tobacco plantation where she was born. Many of the slaves stole away at strange hours of the night and day to a secret spot in the woods. At this sanctified spot, they held illegal prayer meetings to talk about God, in a most plain and sorrowful language. And, they spoke to God in muffled beseeching wails. It was in these meetings that Jenny first heard about Christianity and Jesus Christ, the Son of God, Lord of the universe. And, it was from these meetings that words of hope would filter back throughout the slave population. It was from these meetings that Jenny learned how Jesus died to save her soul. How, if she believed in him, he would prepare a place for her in Heaven. How she would have life everlasting in the hereafter where there were no hardships—only milk and honey. Everything she heard in her mother's hut reaffirmed such notions, but Jenny's reality made this all impossible to comprehend. There was no hope. Even as a child Jenny was unable to perceive hope. God didn't know her and she didn't know God. Jenny had only heard about God, and perhaps, God, had only heard about Jenny. Jenny was faithless and empty. Presently, her only hope, whenever she thought about hope, was with Luis Miguel Matos, the only person on earth who had stirred her.

In her late thirties, Toots Jenny looked sixty. She had brown leathery skin. Her gray speckled hair was unkempt, long and matted. Her teeth were rotten and her eyes were dull with the weight of humiliation. Her back was slouched and she walked with a limp. She mumbled and grinned to herself all day as she went about her chores. She had been treated so cruelly all she awaited now was a gentle death. Or maybe, the unspeakable act. At night up in the attic, she mumbled her outrage and she sent out her signal. Every night in her dreams she saw Luis Miguel Matos and the Black Freighter on the horizon.

One morning, Toots Jenny was jarred awake before dawn by the sound of artillery fire. She briefly thought of Luis Miguel, but it had been more years than she could count since he left and she had all but given up on him. Then she remembered hearing the men talk occasionally about the war. The war to make slavery a permanent institution in the Confederate States of America. Up the river near Port Royal Sound, Fort Walker and Fort Beauregard guarded the entrance to the Port Royal Island and Beaufort. This was from where the sound of the artillery fire came. The repeated blasts from the artillery guns, loud as thunder, woke up everyone. Travis Bouchet, who slept in a back room on the first floor of the Inn, walked out to the tavern pulling up his suspenders. There was great commotion amongst the guest as they came running down to the tavern concerned about what was happening. Everyone knew about the war, but their initial consideration was to be certain that they were not under attack from either the Yankees or the Rebels. Laurent Bouchet and his wife lived in a small house a half-mile inland from the hotel. They traveled a well-worn footpath to the hotel and were the last to gather in the tavern room. Laurent Bouchet, exhibiting his long experience commanding men from his days as a ship captain, took control of the gathering. His assessment was that the fighting was taking place at the mouth of the Sound. Laurent assured everyone that the guns were responding to Yankee gunboats making exploratory probes to test the strength of the fortifications for possible invasion sites. "Alla-us safe so long as the Yankees don't break through," Laurent Bouchet reassured. Then they opened a jug of whiskey and sprawled out at tables drinking and listening to the artillery fire.

Toots Jenny stood at the attic window grinning. Every once in a while she'd see the sky light up, followed by the thunder from the artillery guns. Toots Jenny rocked to the sound and her heart felt light. And, whenever the sky lit up, she grinned joyously. She closed her eyes and wished the artillery fire would come closer. She wanted a direct hit on the hotel—right through her attic roof. The sound of the gun delighted Toots Jenny like nothing else before, but soon there was a lasting quiet and the orange rim of the sun's reflection could be seen rising from the ocean. The Yankee gunboat captains had made their reconnaissance judgements for now. "Toots Jenny'" she heard. It sounded like Travis calling. "Toots Jenny." Toots Jenny readied herself and reported to the kitchen.

Breakfast started earlier this morning than most. Goathead Billy, the freeman cook was boiling oats, breaking eggs, and frying pork. Toots Jenny handed out tin coffee mugs then filled them with watery coffee. Each time the cook called out, she'd go to the kitchen and return with two tin plates of food to serve. There was an uncertainty in the air as the bandits at each table talked about the early morning artillery fire. Those that had a preference sided with the Confederates, but the consensus was that war was bad for their business. With warships patrolling the coast and armies in the fields, it would become impossible for them to carry out their larcenies and return to a secured place unmolested. The Bouchet brothers were concerned that it would become difficult to get fresh provisions. Indeed, would they be allowed to continue to operate untouched? For now, they felt safe as long as their haven went unnoticed by either side. They knew that if the Yankees got control of this area of the coast, they would come up Port Royal Sound and discover the inlet that led to them. That would mean the end. The Rebels would, at the very least, take everything they had and maybe even induct them into the Confederate Army. It was clear that in time they would be obliged to take sides. A group of three outlaws decided they would have their horses saddled up and after breakfast, ride out to learn what they could of the war. Toots Jenny heard everything that was said and although she didn't understand it all, she was exhilarated in what she perceived as their fear and confusion.

Over the next three months, there were sporadic skirmishes and occasional artillery fire, but pirate ships came and left unstopped. Late spring found the guns dormant. The battlefront had moved to other parts of the coast for now. One night a crew of men rowed up to the Hideaway Inn with exciting news. The Confederate Congress had issued a proclamation granting amnesty to any outlaw who enlisted for the Confederate cause. The proclamation allowed President Jefferson Davis the power to offer pardons to wanted men who joined the Southern rebellion against the North. Toots Jenny scrubbed the floor of the tavern and listened carefully as the men talked excitedly and read a tattered copy of the proclamation. The Bouchet brothers, who were old men by now, wanted badly to return to their old stomping grounds in New Orleans. This was an opportunity they never expected, and couldn't pass up. They plotted on how they would sell all of their slaves, sail under the Southern flag, whip the Yankees, and go home to New Orleans free men. And, at that very moment, they started to lay certain plans to relocate.

Toots Jenny felt nauseated that she would be passed on again to another hellhole while these devils escaped the imprisonment of the hunted. Where was the pardon that would free her three brothers, who were sold off when she was a child of four? Where was the pardon to liberate her two sisters? Where was the pardon for the father she never knew? Where was the pardon for her mother who may now reside in the hereafter? Where is the pardon to reunite her with her five sons? And where, oh where, is the pardon for this poor scrubber woman? Night after night, Toots Jenny gave her signal in the window more vigorously then ever, but with a feeling more futile than ever. Then one night as Toots Jenny sent out her signal, she saw a square flash of light that opened and closed in differing intervals: two seconds, four seconds, eight seconds, one second, two seconds, eight seconds. She took her lamp down and thought hard. She knew that she was receiving a signal, but from whom? Could it be Luis Miguel Matos and the Black Freighter? She lifted up her lamp and began to signal again, a small circle, then larger, then larger still, then over and over again. The square flash of light started up again. It was flashing in some systematic manner Toots Jenny could not understand, but it was clearly in response to her signal. For Toots Jenny, the experience felt much like the night Luis talked to her, she couldn't understand much of what was said, but she found meaning following the general tone of the conversation. The general tone of that square flash of light, out there in the darkness, told Toots Jenny something good.

The next morning Toots Jenny reported to the kitchen bright and early. She was dressed real fine. She wore her best frock; an old tattered store bought dress a pirate gave her many years past. She had washed herself and wore a ribbon in her hair. She laughed and grinned like never before. The people who saw her thought Toots Jenny's appearance and attitude this morning just a sign of the advance of her mental affliction. She served their meals, washed the plates, emptied their night pots, made their beds and counted their heads, mumbling unintelligibly, "Nobody's gonna sleep here t'night."

"What she mumbling?" Bandits asked one another throughout the day, "What she got to mumble?"

Toots Jenny felt lightheaded from the power and control she felt. She took fresh drinking water to each room without being told and went about her daily chores with a dignity never before seen. Night came quickly for Toots Jenny. She got to her room a little after ten o'clock, but this night, she never went to bed. She placed her lit lamp in the window and sat next to it. She laid her head in her lap and started a conversation with Jesus Christ. "Jesus, da Christ," Toots Jenny mumbled, "ma time here. Dey da say in dem talks in da wood, have on faith, un lik Christ ded body een de towb, we too, da rise op fom mong de ded. Un 'morrow, great Gawd tey gone fin ma towb emty." Toots Jenny went on in a stream of consciousness until sleep over took her and her talk was replaced with a dream:

A little girl in a sack dress is holding hands with her five sons and turning around and around in a circle in a tobacco field. They are laughing and happy. Then a man comes. He has a dark beard, is dressed in dark clothes, and wears a black hat, and he carries a long whip. He grabs up the boys and the girl turned into a woman as the children cry out to her, their arms reaching and struggling to touch her. The scene replays, only this time, the man takes the girl's brothers and sisters. They are crying out and grabbing for the woman's hand. The woman is in agony. Time passed. The girl, older, is asleep on a cotton mattress in the attic of a large house. The man with the whip comes to her bed. He is drunk. He talks to her, but she doesn't understand what he is saying. He has a jar of whiskey in his hand and when she turns away from him, he throws the whiskey on her, and then he throws himself on her. She fights to resist him. Now he tries to subdue her by biting her ear. And she struggles on for awhile, but she realizes that if she does not submit he will take her ear, and she opens her legs wide. Womanhood, she thinks, what a foul gift, and her mind blanks out all feelings. In the morning, the man gives her an old white flowery dress and she likes the dress, but she never wears it, The girl is a woman again. It is night and her belly is big with child for the fourth time. An old slave woman is summoned to her room. She lay on the cotton mattress and she is in great pain. The old slave woman is coaxing her to push, push, but there is something different in this pregnancy and when one of the baby's feet appears first, the problem becomes clear. The old slave woman calls for the help of another slave woman. And through great agony and unbearable pain, and a miracle, the baby is born and the mother's life is spared. The woman in the dream remembered the moment the baby came free and the sound was that of a loud bang in her mind.

The bang shook Toots Jenny's body and she awakens and hears the bang, bang, of artillery fire. She had given birth to her freedom. The Hideaway was under attack. It was somewhere near four o'clock in the morning and the shells were falling short of the mark. Toots Jenny sat in the window and cried, as she prayed for a direct hit. "Nobody gonna sleep here 'night," she grinned. The population at the compound this morning was twenty-seven whites, one free black man, and twelve slaves. They all began to gather in the tavern. The barrage came closer to shore, then an artillery shell exploded behind the Inn near the slave quarters. The slaves from the quarters came running into the tavern and huddled noisily in a corner. Two of them had been hit and was bleeding. The cook was in his room behind the kitchen. The shells were arriving in two-minute intervals and they crawled closer as if someone was taking a measure of the location. Everyone else, except Laurent Bouchet and his wife were in the tavern. All the white men were armed and they talked strategy to resist any land invasion. They had no idea what force was attacking them; they were only sure that they needed to set up some kind of defense. The bombardment was meant to make them take cover while a land invasion took place, they reasoned. Laurent Bouchet and his wife finally arrived. They were both out of breath and shaky. She took a seat trying desperately to catch her breath, as Laurent took charge-shouting orders to set up a perimeter defense outside

Three hours before the artillery fire began, Luis Miguel Matos, Captain of the Black Freighter, dispatched a detail of fifteen men in a landing boat to make a landing to the right of the mouth of the inlet. The squad of men were to cut their way through the marsh by daybreak and be ready to attack the Hideaway Tavern and Inn from its right flank when they heard evidence of a frontal attack. It was a warm morning with spotty fog and low visibility over the shore of the inlet. Unknown to the Bouchet brothers and their newly formed militia, who were fanned out in defense against a frontal attack, fifteen men from the Black Freighter laid to their right flank, much like a cocked pistol. From the window, in the attic, Toots Jenny watched Laurent Bauchet direct his men into positions behind trees, rocks, an overturned rowboat and whatever gave them concealment and protection.

It wasn't long before three landing boats, each with about six men, could be seen through the fog, slowly making their way towards the shore. The bombardment continued and got heavier as the boats got closer. Laurent ordered his men to hold their fire until the boats got closer. The boats were dispersed and traveled in a winged formation. Laurent directed his men to fire their first volley on the lead boat when he gave the order. The anxiety mounted as the men watched the landing boats come closer and kept themselves concealed. The artillery shells were exploding between the approaching boats and the concealed men on the shore. As the invading boats came closer, the shells fell closer to the shore. Then, if out of nowhere, a shell exploded in a tree where two men had taken up positions, badly wounding one. The wounded man cried out in pain and his sound spooked two others into firing without Laurent's order. The men in the boats returned fire as they rowed closer and now the battle took place. The exchange of gunfire went on for less than a minute before the defenders received gunfire from their right flank. The bombardment stopped as if on cue. With fierce yells and a hail of gunfire, Luis Miguel's men in the woods attacked the surprised garrison from the right flank. The pirates under attack tried to reform their line of defense, but their coordination was clumsy. A few men were dropped by gunshots, trying to reach cover to defend their right flank. There was a heavy volley of gunfire from both sides. The defenders were receiving gunfire from two sides and more of them fell wounded or dead. The Spaniards' that laid in ambush over-ran the outgunned bandits' positions. The Bouchet brother's men were quickly overwhelmed. They surrendered their arms as the attackers moved in from the shore and from the flank. In the last boat to reach the shore was Captain Luis Miguel Matos. He was a majestic figure as he shouted out orders to his men in Spanish, and they quickly disarmed the defeated garrison. Seven men from the Hideaway were dead and eight were wounded. Laurent Bouchet, with a lethal wound to his chest, was among the wounded. The survivors were all made to sit in a row facing the inlet and their hands were tied behind their backs.

Toots Jenny joined the other slaves and Goathead Billy on the lower veranda of the hotel. Laurent's wife ran off into the woods soon as the fighting began. Luis Miguel ordered a detail of his men to guard the captured bandits. Another detail of men was positioned around to secure the area. A third detail of men was ordered to search out and collect everything of value. Luis Miguel and two of his officers approached the veranda. Toots Jenny tried to straighten her back to look her best, but she knew that she looked dreadful and she felt unworthy. Luis Miguel walked up to her and took her hand into his. He looked into her eyes. He kissed her on the cheek, but Toots Jenny could see the disappointment in his eyes. Even so, he treated her with dignity. Luis Miguel had traveled the Americas and saw first hand what the institution of slavery left of the human spirit. "I have returned," he said, in improved English, far superior to Toots Jenny's Gullah, "to make you a subject of the king of Spain." Toots Jenny had no idea what any of that meant, but it felt good. "Now you will come with me," Luis Miguel directed, as he led Toots Jenny to the spot where the tied and captured men sat. "Shall we kill them now or later?" he asked Toots Jenny loudly so the men could hear, as he pointed a pistol towards them. "Shall we kill them now or later?" he repeated as his men busily loaded the boats with looted goods. Toots Jenny rolled the words around in her head. "Speak up," Luis Miguel demanded. "You are in no danger." Toots Jenny remained speechless, her eyes caressing the captured men.

"Look at me," Luis Miguel said to the doomed men, "I am Luis Miguel Matos, Captain of the Black Freighter, an independent ally of the government of Spain. Half of what I get from you goes to the king; the rest belongs to my men and to me. Look there toward the horizon, that is my ship." At the moment while all eyes were on Luis Miguel, a young bandit who had worked his hands free rose and ran off into the woods. A few shots were fired after him, and he may have been hit, but Luis Miguel stopped any pursuit. "Let him go. Someone must tell the tale of the Black Freighter," he said in Spanish. Then he gave an order and soon the hotel and all the buildings on the compound were on fire. Toots Jenny, her throat dry from the excitement, looked into the eyes of Travis Bouchet, the father of two of her sons and softly uttered the word "Now." Then she cleared her throat and said forcefully, "Kill them right now." By twelve-noon the deed was done. Another order from Luis Miguel got his men loaded into the landing boats. The fire on the inlet faded away as the Black Freighter, her sails full, set off into the sun. Toots Jenny, her first time ever off the earth's soil looked back and thought: "That'll learn ya."